MW01128251

ISBN-13: 9781980465157

Also by Blair Howard

The Harry Starke Novels
Harry Starke
Two for the Money
Hill House
Checkmate
Gone
Family Matters
Retribution
Calypso
Without Remorse
Calaway Jones
Emoji
Hoodwinked
The Lt. Kate Gazzara Novels
Jasmine
Saffron
Civil War Series
Chickamauga
The Mule Soldiers
Three Days in Hell
Westerns
The Chase
Comanche

Saffron

A Lt. Kate Gazzara Novel

By

Blair Howard

For Jo As Always

Chapter 1

It was one of those godforsaken nights made even worse by the mantle of rain-sodden mist that swirled within the confines of the narrow alley. The glow of a single streetlight at the entrance to what was optimistically called Prospect Street reflected off the watery surface of the blackened and blistered asphalt and speared the darkness like a glittering finger pointing at something lying on the ground beside the dumpster. What it was T.J. Bron couldn't identify. Not that he tried. Not that he was even interested. He was hungry, had been for as long as he could remember. He was also broke, soaked to the skin, miserable almost to the point of intolerance and wondering if perhaps the time might finally have come when he should end it all.

At that point, he was simply looking for a dry spot to contemplate the method of his own proposed demise. And it was also at that moment when he was blinded by the headlights of a car that appeared out of nowhere and headed toward him at high speed which, considering the confines of the narrow street, and that he couldn't see, alarmed him—no, it scared the shit out him. He flattened himself against the sodden brick wall and the car flashed by, throwing up a wall of water on either side. The driver's side of the car missed him by inches; the wall of icy water did not. For a moment he just stood there, dripping, watching the tail lights until, with a screech of the tires, they made a left turn and disappeared.

He let himself slide down the wall until his backside hit the wet asphalt, and there he sat; cold, wet, and more alone than he'd ever been.

Shit, even Nam was better'n this.

He drew his knees in, wrapped his arms around them, and let his head fall onto them. He was done, had enough. It was time. The only questions that remained were where and how.

He lifted his head, glanced to the left, shook it, then turned to look to the right. The dumpster looked promising. Well, not really, but beggars... *Yeah, that's what I am, a damned beggar. Well, no more.* He felt inside the pocket of the sodden U.S. Army Shell Parka. It was still there, though he wondered if he had the strength in his fingers to open the blade. *Okay, that's the how. A couple of quick slashes—it's cold. Shouldn't feel a thing—an' I'll bleed out in just minutes... yeah! Well, maybe later. Now, let's go take a look at the dumpster.*

He struggled to his feet and shuffled through the darkness and the rain toward what he figured to be his final resting place. *A friggin' dumpster... Hmm, about what I deserve, I suppose.* But as he approached the dumpster the spear point

2

of light from the distant streetlamp again drew his attention to the unidentifiable black bulk lying at its far end. As he drew closer, he saw it was just one of a dozen or so black, plastic garbage bags stacked against the steel sides, or was it? Something about it looked familiar, but... *Ah, who gives a shit?*

Had he been interested enough to take a look, he might have figured it out, but he wasn't. He was tired, soaked to the skin, and wanted nothing more than a dry spot to settle down and— he fingered the pocket knife through the material— *Peace at last, oh Lordy, peace at last.*

Some of the bags were broken open, their contents spewing out onto the street. He stirred them with his foot, wrinkled his nose at the foul smell. *Rotten cabbage? Yeah, that and a whole mess of other putrid crap. No, not here. I ain't much, but I do deserve a little more than to go out with the trash.*

He stirred some more, hoping he might find an edible morsel, but all he found was more rotten food, vegetables and other disgusting, stinking messes dumped by the cooks from the back of the Chinese restaurant across the alley.

He shook his head, dejected, and pulled the hood of the heavy parka tighter over the ancient John Deere ball cap. He pulled down on the bill of the cap so that it covered his eyes and face, protecting them from the pouring rain and then, head down, arms folded across his chest, he shuffled around the end of the dumpster to the tiny open porch at the rear of the Sorbonne, so-called night club and haunt of the deplorables... and sometimes the slumming, smart set of Chattanooga.

He stepped inside, set his back against the steel door and slid down to sit on his haunches in the relative shelter of the porch, let his chin fall to his chest, and closed his eyes. For fifteen, maybe twenty minutes, he simply sat there, half-asleep, thinking, dreaming... remembering. Finally, he sighed, lifted his head, opened his eyes and peered around. He blinked as his eyes adjusted to the darkness of the shadow cast by the dumpster. At first, he could see almost nothing, only the single finger of light from the distant streetlamp that fell upon...

What the hell is *that?* He wondered.

With an effort, he grabbed the steel doorknob, heaved himself upright, and then walked unsteadily to the dumpster. With one hand on the steel side, he steadied himself, leaned down and grabbed the corner of the black plastic wrapping and pulled. The rain-soaked painter's tape gave way, the plastic peeled back, and a pair of dead eyes stared up at him.

"*Oh shit!*" He dropped the edge of the plastic sheet back in place, staggered backward into the porch, then turned and hammered on the steel door with both fists, yelling obscenities. And he kept on hammering until finally the door screeched open a couple of inches and two bleary eyes glared at him through the gap.

"What the hell you doin', T.J.?" Benny Hinkle yelled at him. "It's past three. Get your ass outta here before I kicks it all the way to the damn river." He pushed the door to close it, but T.J. rammed it with his shoulder, knocking Benny backwards into the dimly lit passageway.

"There's a body out there, you fat asshole. I ain't got no phone. Call the damn police, for Chrissake!"

"Body? What body? Lemme see." He rushed out into the rain, to where T.J. was pointing.

"Holy crap," Benny said, as he lifted the corner of the plastic sheet. "I know her. Get your ass in here while I make the call."

"Screw you. I'm outta here." And T.J. turned, but before he could take a step, Benny grabbed him by the arm and hauled him in through the door. Any other time, T.J., an ex-Vietnam vet, would have been too much for him. As it was, T.J. was in bad shape and Benny had little trouble steering him down the passageway and into the empty bar.

He picked up two glasses and a bottle, slammed them down on the bar top, and said, "You pour while I make the call."

Ten minutes later, Prospect Street was ablaze with flashing blue and red lights.

Chapter 2

I was in bed when the call came in. The jangling tone and incessant buzzing of my iPhone dragged me back into the land of the living. I raised myself up on my elbows and stared through my hair at the bedside clock and groaned; it was just after four. I'd been in bed for less than three hours, having spent the hours between eleven and one in the morning following up on a drive-by shooting in East Lake.

I ran my fingers through my hair, pushed it back away from my eyes, and made a wild grab for the phone. I squinted at the display. *Damn!*

I rolled onto my side and tapped the screen. "This better be good, Lonnie," I growled.

"Yeah. I figured as much. Sorry LT. We've got a new one. In the alley behind Benny Hinkle's place. I'm on my way there now."

I flopped back down on the pillows, the phone still at my ear, "Okay. I'll be there as quick as I can." And I hung up before he had a chance to respond.

I dragged myself out of bed, staggered to the window, and stared out. It was raining; the water was coursing down the pane in rivulets. *Damn, damn, damn.*

I took two steps back, sat down on the edge of the bed, put my head in my hands, and wished to die. I sat like that for several moments, then dropped my hands to my knees, shook my head, and rose unsteadily to my feet.

Okay Kate, I thought. *Shower and coffee and you'll feel better.*

Thankfully, I'd set the coffee machine before I went to bed. All I had to do was push the button, and then head for the shower.

It was cold in my apartment. I'd lowered the heat before hitting the sheets. No matter, I turned the shower on cold, took a deep breath, and stepped in. The shock of the icy water would have killed a penguin. I wasn't in there more than ten seconds before I literally leapt out and grabbed a towel. I hurriedly toweled off, my teeth clattering like castanets, my skin a half-acre of goosebumps. I dropped the towel on the floor and headed, naked, for the kitchen. I poured a mug of steaming black coffee, sat down, cradled the cup in both hands, and sipped, relishing the sensation of the scalding, bitter liquid as it coursed down my throat and through my chest.

Any other time, I would've sat and enjoyed the coffee, but I had no time for that. I dressed quickly in jeans, shirt, sweater, and rubber boots. I clipped my holster and badge to my belt, swallowed another quick slug of coffee, slipped into my old Barbour jacket—the damn thing was still wet—grabbed my keys and an already soggy umbrella, and hightailed it out the door.

By the time I arrived at the entrance to Prospect Street, the heavy overnight rain had diminished to a fine drizzle; better, but still cold and uncomfortable.

I parked on the adjoining street, close to the entrance to Prospect, and trudged through the rain, head down, umbrella up, toward the lights and the familiar white canvas tent erected over the body. My partner Lonnie Guest was already there, so were Doc Sheddon, Mike Willis, and at least a dozen uniforms. Even dressed in wet-weather clothing, they looked like a pack of half-drowned rats.

Lonnie held up the tape as I ducked under.

"Welcome to hell," Mike Willis said as we joined them. He moved in close, under the umbrella.

"Yes, you can say that again," I responded, leaning away from him a little; he didn't seem to notice.

"Welcome to..." He caught the look I shot at him and didn't finish. Instead he grinned at me,

I nodded, "Did you recognize her?"

He gave me a kind of shifty-eyed look, glanced up at Lonnie, sighed, and then said, "Yeah. I seen her before. In fact, she was in here earlier, an' she's been in several times before. I made her for some sort o' classy hooker." He shrugged. "Maybe she was, maybe she wasn't. She *was* a good-looking kid, though, dressed nice, too nice for the kind of people we see in this place." He shrugged, "I dunno... She seemed a nice enough kid..." He stared down at the desktop, picked up an invoice, looked at it without seeing, then dropped it and looked up at me. "She was a nice kid," he repeated.

"You say she was in here earlier. What time and who was she with?"

He thought for a minute, and then said, "Just after ten, I think. I didn't take a whole lot of notice. I probably wouldn't have noticed her at all if it'd been the weekend. As it was, it was kinda slow. She was on her own, at first. Two or three guys tried to hit on her, but she was having none of it. That's about all I saw. I came back here to check some invoices. You can ask Laura. She was here; she always is."

He was talking about his long-time partner, Laura Davies. They run the Sorbonne between them. It's a strange, symbiotic relationship that they have. A more incongruous couple I have never come across, but it works.

"I can do that," I said. "When would be a good time?"

"Any time after four."

I nodded, "What was she wearing, Benny, did you notice?"

He shrugged, "Jeans, boots, and one of them big ol' parka coats—dark green, I think, with a brown collar—an' dark red sweater under it... Could have been brown, I suppose."

"What time did she leave, and who with?"

"I didn't see her leave. Again, you'll need to talk to Laura."

"Come on, Benny, think about it, for God's sake. You said she was alone at first, that meant she was with someone later, so you must've seen that someone. Was it a man, woman? Did you know him, or her?"

"Well, yeah, okay. There was one guy. An older guy, older than her, at least. Look, I told ya, I really didn't take a whole lot of notice. He was just... He was just, well, ordinary. He bought her a drink, I think."

"Oh, for God's sake," Lonnie said, as he pushed himself away from the door and walked to the desk.

He leaned forward, put both hands on the desk top, and said, "How the hell old was he, Benny? Thirty, thirty-five, forty, what?"

"I dunno," he leaned back in his chair, rolled it away from the desk, away from Lonnie. "I don't know. Thirty-five, maybe forty?"

"That's better. What was he wearing?"

"Jeans..." He stared up at the ceiling, his eyes half-closed.

"Come on, Benny. Think. You're not that dense."

"Jeans..." he repeated. "No. Dark pants... maybe. I dunno; a plaid shirt, red and black, I think, and one of those big puffy quilted coats... Black... It was black."

Lonnie walked around the desk and parked his backside on the edge. Benny rolled his chair even further away until it hit the iron bedstead and would go no further.

"Describe him, Benny," Lonnie said, leaning toward him.

"Oh shit, Lonnie, I don't know. I told ya, I didn't take a good look at him, honest... Brown hair. He was wearing a ball cap, a black ball cap. He was maybe five-eight, five-ten... I don't know. Heavyset, but maybe that was just the jacket. I'm telling you. That's all I know. Look, I need to get some damn sleep, so if you don't mind..."

"And that's it..."

"That's enough, Lonnie," I said. I was tired and in no mood to listen to any more of Benny's whining, or Lonnie trying to browbeat him.

Lonnie turned and glared at me, his eyebrows raised in question. I shook my head. He shrugged and stood upright on his feet.

"Okay, Benny," I said, as I rose and rubbed my aching butt. Cold steel will do that to you. "I get it. You know nothing, like always. If you think of anything else, call me. You have my number. Come on, Lonnie. Let's get out of here."

I turned towards the door, but then looked back at him.

"Hey, whadda ya mean, like always?" He looked chastened. "I always try to help law enforcement... Especially you, Kate. You know that."

"Yes, sometimes." I held up my hand to stop the inevitable protest. "Just tell Laura that we'll be in to see her this afternoon, okay?"

26

"Yeah. I'll tell her. You have a good day, y'heah?"

***

It was almost nine o'clock when we left the Sorbonne that morning, and it was raining again.

"Tell you what, Lonnie," I said as I opened the cruiser door and slid inside, "I'm so tired I can't see straight. Let's go talk to this J.J. character and then go home and get a couple hours of sleep. I don't think we're going to learn anything from him, but we can at least go through the motions. What do you say?"

He nodded, "T.J., you mean... Whatever you say, LT. Whatever you say."

27

Chapter 4

I'd never met T.J. Bron before, but I'd heard of him: the man was a war hero. At least he had been... He'd been awarded some sort of medal for bravery, I think I heard. Anyway, back then he was living on the streets, on hand-outs. Had done so for as long as anyone could remember. He'd been in and out of one shelter or another since he lost his home during the subprime mortgage debacle in 2008. *Ten years... He's been wandering the streets for ten years. That's damn sad. He deserves better than that.*

He was a big man: big hands, clasped together on the steel table top; big head, red face— probably due to the weather—gray hair and beard, both long and unkempt, and the most beautiful pale-blue eyes. He was wearing several layers of clothing: I could see at least two grubby jackets under the worn-out US Army parka. He looked cold... and lost.

"T.J.? Is it okay if I call you T.J.?"

He looked up at me and nodded. There was something about his eyes, a lost look, hopelessness.

I looked up at the clock on the wall. It was just after nine-thirty. I knew he must have been sitting there for several hours. *Not even a cup of damned coffee. Well, I'll see about that.*

28

I turned to Lonnie, "Do me a favor, will you?" I asked quietly. "Go and get this man something to eat and some coffee."

He looked at T.J., then nodded. "How about a couple of sausage'n egg biscuits, T.J.?"

The man nodded, seemed to brighten up a little, then dropped his head and stared at his hands.

"You okay?" I asked, as I sat down opposite him; I heard Lonnie close the interview room door behind him.

He looked up at me, a spark of what I took to be anger in his eyes.

"Yeah. I'm fine. Just fine. Who the hell are you, and when can I get the hell outta here? I got things to do." The sarcasm in his voice hit me like a fist.

"I'm Lieutenant Gazzara. I work homicide... This homicide... Tell you what, let's get out of here, go somewhere a little warmer, then we can talk." I got up. He stayed put.

"This'll do fine. I ain't gonna be here long. What's to talk about? All I did was find her."

I sat down again, thought for a minute, then said, "Okay, so we'll stay here... Look, T.J., I know it's none of my business, but what the hell happened to you? You had a wife, a house, a job..."

"Yeah," he interrupted me. "I had it all," he said, bitterly. "And you're right, it ain't none of your damned business..." He paused, glared across the steel table at me, then seemed to relax; his look softened.

"I lost my job. I was fired... for stealing... only I never stole a damn thing. Someone did, but not me. I have a degree in Corporate Finance, would you believe? I was a loan officer at one of the Hartwell Community Banks. Almost a half mil disappeared out of a customer's account..." He shrugged.

"Look at me for God's sake. Does it look like I got away with that kind of money?" He grinned wryly at me. "They couldn't prove it was me—it wasn't—but they fired me anyway, and I became unemployable. My wife walked out on me, and Hartwell foreclosed on my house—their way of getting some of their money back, I suppose..."

Just then, the door opened and Lonnie walked in with one of those pulp-fiber coffee trays from McDonald's—there's one just across the road from the PD.

Bless him. He'd brought coffee—large ones—for all of us, and I sure as hell needed a caffeine jolt. He handed the cups around and placed two small packages in front of T.J., who grabbed one, tore it open, and took a huge bite, closed his eyes and chewed slowly, seemingly savoring every last crumb.

Lonnie sat down next to me and we sipped our coffee, watching him as he ate, which he did with some reserve, making no noise and no mess. The man still had his dignity and had retained his good manners, regardless of his time on the streets.

We waited until he'd finished and then I said, quietly, "What were you doing in that alley at three o'clock in the morning, T.J.?"

He sighed, stared down at the coffee cup now cradled in both hands, then looked up at me and said, "What do you think? I'm a bum, Lieutenant. Homeless. A waste of skin; a blot on society; not worth the cost of a cup of coffee," he said, bitterly. "I'm sorry. I didn't mean you guys. Thank you for *your*... contribution." He paused, his elbows on the table, sipped, and seemed to contemplate his fingers wrapped around the coffee cup in front of his face. Then he continued, "To answer your question, I was just about at the end of my rope... looking for a dry spot to try to get some sleep and to... Well, we don't need to talk about that. Anyway, in the light of the street lamp, I saw the black bundle beside the dumpster. It looked kinda weird, so I took a look... and I got the shock of my life. I've seen a lot of death, but those eyes… I'll never forget them, never."

"Did you touch anything?" Lonnie asked.

"No, sir. Well, just the edge of the plastic wrapper."

"And then… what?"

"Hell. I panicked. I hammered on the door. Benny opened it, finally… He called you guys. That's it. There's no more."

Did you see anything in the alley, anybody sneaking around, parked cars or trucks?" Lonnie asked.

"No. Nothing. No…one. Well, there was a car, but it wasn't parked. It was going pretty fast; almost hit me."

"And when was that?" I asked, ignoring the thrill his answer gave me.

"Just a few minutes before I found her."

"What type of car? Did you get the license plate?" Lonnie asked, his stylus poised over his iPad.

T.J. shook his head, "No. I didn't look at the plate. Water from the tires hit me in the face. I was soaked. But it was an SUV of some sort, an older model. I think it might have been a Ford." Then he grinned, and the change was dramatic: T.J. Bron was a good-looking man. "Then again, it might have been a Chevy." The smile disappeared. "It was a dark color, not black... Definitely not black. Red, maybe. Brown. Maroon. Might even have been blue. It was moving really fast. Headlights on full beam, right at me. I jumped out of the way and it sped past me, and was gone. I barely saw a glimpse of it."

"How about the driver?" Lonnie asked. "Did you get a look at him?"

"No. I told you: high-beam headlights then a face full of water. Sorry."

"That's okay," I said. "We have more now than we did—an older model SUV, possibly dark red or dark blue."

"Sounds like a Bronco, or a Blazer, or maybe a GMC Jimmy," Lonnie said, thoughtfully. "What d'you think, T.J.?"

"Could be. As I said, I didn't get a good look, but what you're saying sounds about right."

He sighed. "That it? I need to go to the shelter; see if I can get dried out some." He held out the lapels of his parka. He was right. His clothes were soaked.

"Yes, that's it for now. I'll have somebody take you down there..." I looked at his face, "Hey?"

33

He looked at me through empty eyes. I knew what he was thinking... At least I thought I did, and it wasn't good.

Damn! Somebody needs to give this guy a break... And then I had a thought. *Hmmm. I wonder if... Nah! But what was it my ol' dad said: If you don't ask, you don't get. Okay then. He can only say no!*

"Listen, T.J., I might be able to help... at least I know someone who... might... If I..."

"What d'you mean, help? You can't help me. Nobody can. I'm screwed, forever. If I hadn't found that girl, I'd be dead right now. It would have been my body they found beside that dumpster. No, sister, you can't help me. Now, just show me the way out and leave me be." He started to rise from the seat.

"T.J., what have you got to lose by talking to him? Let me call him. Just talk to him... please?"

He stared at me, half out of his seat.

"Please?"

He sighed, shook his head, sat down again, then said, "Okay, go for it."

I smiled, took my phone from my pocket, hit the speed dial, put it to my ear, and waited.

"Hey, Kate. It's been a while. What's up?"

"Hello, Harry. Yes, it has… Look, I need a favor. Where are you? I need to talk to you."

"I'm at the office. Come on over. I have some Dark Italian Roast and the fire's all aglow. Fifteen minutes?"

"I'll be there, but it'll be more like forty-five minutes to an hour and… Umm, I'll have someone with me. That okay?"

"Sure. We have plenty of cups. See you soon, then."

"Thanks, Harry."

"My pleasure." And he hung up.

"Harry," T.J. said. "Who the hell is Harry?"

"Harry Starke…"

"Hah! No way. I know that guy. He used to be a cop but now he's a PI. He's loaded, right?"

"He's quite wealthy, yes."

"Look, lady, there's nothing a guy like that can do for me. I'm not looking for a handout."

"And you won't get one. I happen to know he's looking for an investigator; corporate finance."

"Hah! And you think he'll hire me? Fat chance. I'm a homeless bum, remember? Besides... look at me.

I nodded, "Yes, we need to get you cleaned up a bit. Lonnie, why don't you take him down to the locker room. Let him take a shower. Maybe you can find him something dry to wear, for now at least. You're about his size, right?"

"No, no, no, no... no!" T.J. objected.

"Yeah. I might be able to find something. Let's go, brother."

They arrived back at my office less than thirty minutes later. T.J. Bron looked like a different person. He was wearing clean jeans—a little too big for him, but serviceable enough—and a denim shirt under a thick black wool sweater, and a short black rain slicker to replace his parka. His hair and beard were shiny clean and combed. Even his attitude was brighter. He was standing tall, his back stiff, shoulders back. I was impressed.

"I don't know about this, Lieutenant," he said as I stood up and put my coat on. "He's not going to hire me. Why would he? I haven't been in the business for more than ten years. I've forgotten all I once knew."

"You can get help with that. Let's go talk to the man. We've nothing to lose. One thing, though.

Be straight with him. Tell him nothing but the truth. If you don't, he'll know. He's uncanny that way."

Chapter 5

We, the three of us, arrived at Harry's office on Georgia Avenue at just after eleven that morning. Lonnie parked the cruiser in Harry's lot. We dodged the rain and entered in a rush through the side door, much to Jacque Hale's surprise—her hand flew to her desk drawer, where I knew she kept a Glock 43.

"Oh, m'God," she said when she realized who had just burst in on her. Don't do that, Kate. I could have shot you."

"Not you, Jacque," I laughed. "Anyone else, but not you. You're too savvy."

I looked around the office; Jacque was on her own.

"Where's the boss? He's expecting us."

"Yes, I know. I'll tell him you're here."

She picked up the phone, punched a button, and said, "Harry, Kate's here." She listened, nodded, and put the handset back in its cradle, then looked up at me and said, "Go on through. I'll have Jessica bring coffee."

"Thanks, Jacque," I said, then, "Lonnie, I need you and T.J. to give me a few minutes alone with Harry. I need to explain what's going on and what I have in mind."

"I'll get you some coffee," Jacque said.

"That's okay," Lonnie said, "I know where it is. C'mon T.J."

Jacque nodded, then turned to look at me, "Jessica has already taken yours in."

I took a deep breath, looked at Jacque and mouthed, *"Wish me luck."* Then I stepped to the door to Harry's office...

I hadn't seen him in more than a month, not since that Jim Wallace debacle. Yes, that one. It was all over the TV and the newspapers. That was one Harry got wrong, a rarity for him. I'd warned him off, several times but, Harry being Harry, he took no notice and got his butt handed to him. He fixed it, of course, but it was a mess.

I knocked on the door and pushed it open. He was sitting behind his desk. He stood and grinned at me.

"It's about time," he said as he came around the desk and hugged me. He stepped away, and said, "Where the hell have you been? I was going to call you, but..." He paused, smiled sheepishly at me, then continued, "I figured you must be mad at me—the Wallace case."

So, he didn't blame me. That's good.

Harry and I go back a long way, since I was a rookie cop more than seventeen years ago. I was his partner for eight years, until he left the force and went into business for himself. And... we were lovers once, a long time ago... well, three years anyway. Now we're just good friends... at least we were until the Wallace thing. Now? I hope so. We've worked together, on and off, over the years since he quit the PD. It's been a semi-official arrangement, with the reluctant blessing of Chief Johnston—he and Harry never really got along—but the chief likes to get something for nothing and Harry, probably the best homicide investigator in the southeast, usually doesn't come cheap, much less for free. But that's what we get, Harry's expertise on a consultative basis and it doesn't cost the city a dime. This time, though, it was me needing a favor... well, for T.J.

"Your coffee," he pointed to the cup and saucer on the table in front of the great stone fireplace. "It's getting cold."

He sat down on the couch on one side and I sat on the other, facing him across the table.

"How's Amanda? Still doing well, I hope?"

"Oh yeah. You know her. Nothing phases her."

"Do you know what's she's having yet?"

"Yeah, a baby," and he laughed out loud, then said, "No. And we don't want to."

He grabbed his mug—no wimpy cup for him—and leaned back into the leather upholstery, "It's good to see you, Kate."

I nodded, "So all is forgiven?"

He pulled a face, "There's nothing to forgive. If I hadn't been so bloody single-minded, I'd have seen it for myself. What a damned mess. Still, it all came out right in the end." He paused and set his mug on the table. "So, you said you needed a favor. What can I do for you?"

I sipped my coffee. It was sooo good. I looked at him and smiled, "It's... not for me... well, it is, but... Look, Lonnie's outside with someone I'd like you to meet. He's had some bad breaks and needs a hand up. I sort of thought you..."

I saw the look on his face. Skeptical didn't describe it.

"Oh, stop it," I said. "He's a good guy that's gone, is going, through some rough times. He has a degree in corporate finance and I know you need an investigator to replace Ronnie, so it won't hurt you to at least talk to him. You might even know him. He worked for Hartwell, until they fired him."

"Hmmm. Hartwell Community Banks. That brings back memories."

He was referring to a case we worked together a couple of years ago. I smiled at him, "We've had some good times together, you and I."

He nodded, "That we have," and then he winked at me. I really wasn't sure what that meant, but I could guess. I ignored it.

"So," I said. "Will you talk to him? He needs cleaning up a bit, but I think you could do a whole lot worse."

"He's outside, you say?"

"Yes."

He stood, walked to the door, opened it and said, "Jacque, show them in please."

I stood and made the introductions. Lonnie, he already knew, of course. In fact, they'd attended the police academy together.

"Lonnie," Harry said, extending his hand. "It's been a while..." He turned and said, "T.J. Bron. I know you, T.J., at least I've heard of you. Distinguished Service Cross, two purple hearts, right?"

T.J. looked away, embarrassed. Harry looked at me and said, "I think T.J. and I can take it from here. I'll call you later."

And that was as close to the bum's rush out of Harry's office that I've ever come, but it didn't hurt a bit. T.J. was in good hands.

I slammed the cruiser door closed and reached for my seat belt. Lonnie thumbed the starter, put the car in reverse, paused, knocked it into neutral, then turned to me and said, "What do you think? Will Harry give him a job?"

I shrugged, "You never can tell. Tough as he is, he has a soft heart—for God's sake don't tell him I said that."

Lonnie grinned, "You miss him, don't you, Kate? You had a good thing going, you two... until..."

"That's enough, Lonnie," I interrupted him. "It was a long time ago and, well... It was a long time ago."

He nodded, reversed the car away from the building, then drove through the gate onto Georgia, heading west.

I sat quietly for a moment, thinking about what he'd said.

He's right. We did have a good thing going, too good... damn you, Harry Starke. Damn you all to hell.

Involuntarily, I shook my head, trying to rid

myself of the thoughts. Lonnie caught it, but said nothing. I looked at my watch.

"It's almost eleven-thirty," I said. "I need a break. Let's go get a few hours of sleep, yes?"

He nodded.

"Okay then, we're not that far from my place. You want to drop me there and pick me up later?"

"I can do that. What time?"

I looked again at my watch, "Let's say four-thirty. That's almost five hours, plenty of time for a shower and a nap. Laura gets into the Sorbonne at four, so she'll have time to do her thing before we get there."

"Sounds like a plan."

"You'll pick me up at four-thirty, then?"

"That I will."

Chapter 6

When Lonnie dropped me off, I headed for the kitchen, ate a bite or two of cold chicken salad on crackers, gulped down a glass of pomegranate juice, then headed for the bedroom where I flopped facedown on the bed, fully clothed. I would have gone out like that had not my phone rang as I was stretching to place it on nightstand. I looked at the screen. It was Harry.

"Hey, you busy?"

"Oh hell no. I was just about to grab a nap. What's up, Harry?"

"Your boy, T.J. I thought you might like to know. I turned him over to Jacque. She's going to clean him up, buy him some clothes and find him a room. I'm taking a bit of a chance, but I don't think he did what he was accused of. You and I both know what the Hartwells were. Anyway, I'll give him a shot. If he screws up, my bad. If not, we win all round. And you're right, with a military record like his, he deserves a break. I just thought you'd like to know. Now get some sleep. Call me later, if you want to." And he hung up.

I smiled, set the phone down, rolled over onto my back, put my hands behind my head, closed my eyes, and then... the world ended. At least, that's how it seemed when, almost four hours later, the alarm in my phone blasted out La Bamba and I woke from a deep, deep sleep.

I rolled off the bed, landed on my knees, grabbed the phone and turned it off. I looked at the screen; it was three-thirty. I rolled over onto my back on the floor. I felt like... Well, I'm sure you know what I felt like. I rose unsteadily to my feet, staggered to the bathroom, and turned on the shower, hot. Then I stripped, flinging my clothes on the floor, and stepped in. The blistering water hit me like a hammer. I was instantly fully awake and scrabbling for the shower faucet. I turned it down to an almost bearable scalding hot, and then I just stood there, eyes closed, and let the water wash all my cares away... Yeah, right!

Lonnie was right on time. He texted me that he was outside, waiting. I looked out of the window. The cruiser was at the curb; the rain was falling by the bucketful. I sighed, went to the closet and pulled out an ex-Navy P-coat I hadn't worn in years. It was heavy, waterproof, and warm. I looked like crap in it, but what the hell did I care? Winter in Tennessee can be a bitch.

Laura Davies is quite a character. An attractive, busty blonde with an infectious personality, she's usually dressed in a tight-fitting tank vaguely reminiscent of the Hooter's brand, cut-off jeans that barely cover her amazing backside, and the inevitable cowboy boots. The lady is the epitome of the stereotypical Southern barkeep and claims, among other things, to own the longest pair of legs in the city and I for one don't doubt that she does. I've known her for more than fifteen years and count her as one of my few real friends.

I've heard her called everything from a ho to a skank to a slag; she's none of those things. She's a good-hearted woman and she doesn't have a two-timing man. In fact, she has a very understanding husband of more than fifteen years and a couple of kids. The way she dresses and acts when at work is all part of her workplace persona, and he knows it; hell, he even approves. That tank and the cut-offs, they net her more in tips than if she was on a banker's salary.

That day, the tank was a long-sleeved, midnight-blue satin affair. The cut-offs had been replaced by skin-tight black leather pants. The boots had gone too, replaced by three-inch black heels. Her hair, the roots recently dyed, was tied back in a ponytail: I suddenly had a vision of Olivia Newton John in the movie *Grease*. Damned if Laura didn't look almost as good.

"Hey, Kate, Lonnie," she said. "Benny said you might drop by. He's in his office." She rolled her eyes. "If you can call it that. You want to see him?"

"No. It's you we came to see. D'you have a minute?"

She looked slowly around the empty bar, then said, "What d'you think? Ain't like we're rushed off our feet, now is it?"

She came out from behind the bar, "Let's sit in one of the booths. It'll be quieter there," and she giggled. "Though, it couldn't be any quieter than it is right now, now could it?"

Lonnie slid into the booth. I slid in beside him. Laura slithered in on the other side of the table, facing us, her leather pants squeaking on the shiny plastic seat.

"Must get these pants lubed," she said slyly, looking at Lonnie. He grinned back at her but said nothing.

"Okay. I'm here. This is about the body T.J. found last night, right?"

"Yes," I nodded, "but it was at three ayem this morning. Benny said she was in here last night but he remembered very little of her. He said you might."

"Yeah, I remember her. Pretty girl, about twentyish, maybe a little older, light brown hair, highlighted... nice cut, expensive. I could tell that. She was maybe five-six, nice figure."

"Benny said he thought she might have been a hooker," Lonnie said.

"I don't think so. She was well educated... well, she spoke nice, and her clothes were... ordinary? Not cheap, but ordinary. If she *was* a hooker, she hadn't been one very long. I can pick 'em out a mile away, so can you, I bet."

"What was she wearing?"

She pulled a face and shrugged, "Jeans, tan boots, a burgundy turtleneck sweater, and a huge parka—almost to her knees—with a fur collar, dark green."

"So Benny remembered it correctly then; that's a first. How about the guy she was with?" Lonnie asked. "Did you get a look at him?"

"No... Not really. He came in late, had a couple of drinks, which she ordered; they talked for a while, heads together, she was giggling, like they were lovers, almost, then they upped and left."

"So she knew him then?" Lonnie asked

"I'd say so, yes."

"Can you describe him?" I asked.

"What he was wearing? I think so. I never did get a good look at his face. Now I think about it, that might have been intentional... He was wearing a ball cap, a black one. Dark brown hair, medium build, five-ten, maybe, tan pants, red and blue plaid shirt, and a navy-blue coat: one of those puffer jackets. That's about all I can tell you."

Lonnie was checking his notes on his iPad, "Damn, Laura. Aside from the ball cap, that's about as different from how Benny described him as it could be. You sure you got it right?"

She rolled her eyes, "Now who you gonna trust, Lonnie? Benny or me? You know what a ditz he is. Says the first thing comes into his head."

That wasn't entirely true. Benny had come through for us many times in the past, but I did know where she was coming from and, yes, I'd trust her woman's eye for clothing more than I would Benny's.

I nodded, "Has he been in before?"

"I don't think so. If he has, I've not seen him."

"How about the girl?" I asked.

She nodded, "Yes, two or three times, usually with friends... students, I think. You know the type: rowdy, half-drunk, stupid, though that wasn't her. She seemed quite cool-headed." She thought for a moment, then continued, "You know,

now I think about it, she always left quite early, with someone, but never the same someone."

"So, she could have been a working girl, then?" I asked.

"She could, I suppose, but as I said, mostly she was with kids just like her; from UT, I should think, or maybe Chatt' State. We get a lot of them, usually late an' on weekends. Weekdays, it's usually just the lowlifes, the bums, like... well, I hate to say it, like T.J., but not as down and out as him, although Benny does have a soft spot for vets. He was in Vietnam, you know."

"What?" I asked. "Benny? No, I didn't know. Wow, that's one for the books. Benny, a soldier. Wow!"

"He was a corps man, a medic, actually. Had a rough time of it, so I heard, though not from him."

I nodded, "So what time did they leave?"

"I'm not sure... just after ten... ten-fifteenish. I didn't pay a lot of attention."

"Benny said she was alone when she came in," Lonnie said.

Laura nodded, "That's right. Now I did notice that. It was around nine. We were quiet. It never gets busy much before ten, even on

51

weekends. Anyway, she came in, by herself, sat at the bar, that end," she pointed, "and ordered a gin and tonic. She hadn't been here but a few minutes before a couple of guys decided to hit on her. She wasn't having any of it, though. She refused to talk to them. They soon got tired of it and left her alone.

"Whoa, wait a minute," I said. "She ordered a gin and tonic. Did you check her ID?"

She smiled, "That I did, Lieutenant."

"So, you must know her name."

She nodded, "Yes, I remember it because it was unusual, pretty; her first name was Saffron. I don't remember her last name, but she was old enough to drink. I wouldn't have served her otherwise," she winked at Lonnie. He grinned back at her.

One thing I did know. They, Benny and Laura, were very savvy when it came to underage drinking. They didn't allow it, not at all.

So, now we had a name, and we knew the girl was at least twenty-one years old.

"Saffron, huh?" I asked.

She nodded.

"Well, it's a start," I said, turning to look at Lonnie.

"Call Missing Persons. Maybe we'll get lucky; maybe someone's turned in a report."

He nodded and fished his iPhone from his pants pocket and hit the speed dial for the PD.

I stood. So did Laura.

"Thanks for your help, Laura," I said. "It's not much, but it's better than we had. If you remember anything else, you have my number, right?"

"I do. You want a drink before you go?"

I have to tell you, I was tempted. I felt like... well, I wasn't feeling my best, that's for sure. I looked at my watch. It was almost six o'clock. Officially, I was off duty, but...

"No thanks, better not. I never know when I might get called in to work. They're knocking people off like it's a competition, or something. I can't remember the last time I had a full night to myself."

I turned to see how Lonnie was doing. He'd just finished the call. He looked up at me and shook his head. Oh well, maybe tomorrow.

We said our goodbyes and left the club. *Did I really call it that, a club?*

It was already dark outside and still raining. I pulled my P-coat around me, shivering. It was hard to button the damned thing. I guess it must have shrunk. Either that or I'd put on weight. *The hell I have!*

Lonnie pushed the starter and set the climate control to clear the fogged windows, and we just sat there, waiting. Neither of us spoke. Me, I was out of it, my mind elsewhere as I watched the rain coursing down the windshield. The forecast predicted by Channel 7 indicated there wouldn't be any letup until the early morning. It was going to be a wild night. Little did I know how wild.

"Let's get out of here," I said. "I need to eat and sleep. We've the post mortem to attend in the morning and I need to be in a whole lot better shape than I am now."

"Yeah," he said, as he put the car into drive. "About that. How would you feel if I gave it a miss?"

"The post?" I shrugged. "Yes, okay, I suppose. You all right, Lonnie?"

"Will you stop asking me that? Yes, I'm okay. I just hate autopsies, and this one... Well, I can do without that kind of a start to the day. So thanks, I'll go into the office then. Maybe by that time someone will have submitted a report. Your car's at Amnicola, right?"

I nodded.

I drove home that night and parked the car in my garage. It was almost seven o'clock when I entered my kitchen. It was cold in there. In my rush to leave earlier, I'd forgotten to turn up the heat. Fortunately, I had a gas furnace. I set the thermostat to seventy-five and headed for the shower. I'd barely gotten dried off when my iPhone rang. *Oh no. Please, please, no!*

But it was. There'd been another drive-by shooting, on Barnett Avenue. This time a three-year-old girl had died. The bullet had gone clean through the wall of the house and hit her in the head as she was sitting with her mother watching TV. *What the hell was the kid doing out of bed at that time of night?*

I sighed, struggled into some dry clothes, covered myself in an old plastic slicker, and headed out into the night, and the unrelenting rain.

Chapter 7

I missed not seeing Lonnie's car when I arrived in the parking lot at the rear of the Forensic Center. It's on Amnicola, just a couple of blocks from the PD. Fortunately, the rain had stopped, and the clouds were far enough apart to see patches of blue between them. Nice, but winter was a long way from done.

I entered the building through the rear and was met in the receiving area by Carol Oats, Doc Sheddon's Jill-of-all-trades—by profession she's a forensic anthropologist, but due to budget shortages she filled a lot of gaps.

"Hey, Kate. How are you doing? Well, I hope. Doc's not here yet, but he shouldn't be long. Mike's already in there waiting for you, chomping at the bit. You can suit up and go on in. You know where everything is."

I did as she suggested. I suited up and pushed through into the autopsy room. As Carol had said, Mike Willis was ready to rock and roll. He was dressed from head to toe in white Tyvek. A blue paper mask covered his mouth and he had a green surgical cap on his head. Even more incongruous was the weird-looking set of goggles perched atop his head. But that wasn't all. Almost all of the lights were off. He was standing beside the autopsy table, in semi-darkness. From the light of the open door, I could see Mike had his left hand wrapped around the handle of a large, square box-like something, and from his right hand dangled what I took to be its power pack: the two units were connected by a long black cable. He looked like he'd just stepped out of a 1950s sci-fi movie.

"Ah, there you are," he said, placing both units on a small, portable stainless-steel cart that was near the autopsy table upon which lay the naked body of the Jane Doe. *Now known as Saffron.*

"Come on in. We need to get this done. Doc wants to get started at ten, so…"

"New toy, Mike?" I asked.

As soon as I asked the question, I knew I'd made a mistake. Mike likes to talk and I just handed him the prime opportunity.

He grinned like a little boy with a new video game, "Yeah. It arrived last week. This is the first chance I've had to try it out." He picked up the power pack and set it on the floor. Then he held the unit itself out for me to see. "It's a Crime-lite, the latest technology in portable forensic lights. It's made in the UK and it's awesome. This baby can find just about anything anywhere on everything, no matter how small." He waved it in the air, looked up at it proudly, then continued, "It can illuminate a whole room—blood spatter, you know—or just a tiny area, no more than a few square inches."

I tried to look suitably impressed but, well, I wasn't; not really. New technology was arriving every day. What did impress me was that it looked expensive and that he'd been able to persuade the CPD to purchase one for him. There was little enough in the budget for the everyday running of the department, let alone fancy new gadgetry. Still, there it was, and Mike obviously was in one of his "blind 'em with science" moods.

Best let him get it off his chest, I suppose.

"Okay," I said. "I'll bite. How is it different from your old Luma-Lite?"

"Well." He tilted the unit so he could look at its face, "First of all, the light source is ninety-six LEDs, so it's a lot brighter, lighter and handier, and it's a whole lot more sensitive. It can detect blood, fingerprints, semen, tiny hairs, fibers, gunshot residue, and even drugs. It's a really neat tool."

"Yeah, I know what it is and how it does it: you shine the light on a body, floor, wall, bed linen, whatever, and it will show blood spatter and fingerprints and such, right?"

58

"Yeah, I don't know if you know much about light, but various materials absorb and reflect light differently, and to a greater or lesser degree."

Oh dear. Here we go.

"Light, as you may or may not know," he continued, gazing fondly down at his new love, "is measured in wavelengths with ultra-violet light having the shortest wavelength and infra-red the longest. So, by adjusting it to emit different wavelengths... okay, colors, it will reveal stains, fibers, and other evidence that would otherwise be invisible under ordinary artificial or daylight conditions." He glanced at the body on the table. "If there's anything there, we'll find it. Here, put these on. I only have the one spare set. I hope Doc won't want them when he gets here."

He handed me what looked like a set of welder's goggles with a single rectangular blue lens. It was identical to the one he had on his head. I put them on and the world turned blue.

"We'll begin with the feet and work our way up to the head and then flip her over, yeah?"

I shook my head, then said, "Yes, Mike."

"Okay, so come close and follow the light. Maybe if I miss anything, you'll spot it."

I did as I was asked and some twenty minutes later—it seemed to me like a couple of hours—he was playing the light on her head, gently riffling his gloved fingers through her hair.

He hadn't found very much, just a few strands of hair, a dozen or so small fibers, and two minute scraps of something white; all of which were bagged and tagged and signed off on as we went.

He finished with her hair and we turned her over so that she was facedown on the autopsy table, and we started over. It was a time-consuming task and when we were done, my back was aching from all of the bending. What did we have? More hairs, fibers, and white stuff.

Finally, the ordeal was over. I was exhausted. Not so Mike. He took the goggles from me, packed up his equipment—handling it fondly—gathered together the evidence baggies, and promised to call me later with the results. Then he left, whistling cheerfully to himself. *Good for him, I suppose. Me? Now I have it all to go through again with Bilbo.*

Just as I finished the thought, Bilbo Baggins himself entered the chamber, dressed and ready to wreak havoc on the poor girl now resting quietly, faceup, on the table.

"Hiya, Kate," Doc Sheddon said, rubbing his gloved hands together as he advanced through the plastic swinging doors. He was dressed in green scrubs, mask, cap, and a huge, incongruously huge, face shield—it reminded me of a welder's mask—tilted back above his head.

"Let's do this," he said. And he did. He flipped the shield down in front of his face, picked up a scalpel, waved it in the air like a conductor, and... I'm not going to assault your senses by describing what happened next. It's bad enough for me that I had to go through it once, much less repeating it here. So, suffice it to say, the next ninety minutes were harrowing, as they always are.

Finally, he stepped back, shoved the face shield up and over his head, stripping it off. He laid it down beside the set of stainless-steel bowls that now contained the poor girl's liver, brain, heart, kidneys, the contents of her stomach, and... well, you get the idea.

"So," he said, as he pulled the overhead microphone down, peeling off his gloves and mask, and began to record his findings. "The body is that of a normally developed white female. Height, five feet eight inches; weight, one hundred and twenty-three pounds. Age is estimated to be between eighteen and twenty-five..."

I listened to him, but I didn't really hear anything, if you can understand that. I sighed and shook my head as he droned on, and on, and on interminably.

"Lividity is fixed in the distal portions of the limbs, and in the back and buttocks. The eyes are open. The irises are brown and corneas are cloudy. Petechial hemorrhaging is present in the conjunctival surfaces of the eyes, eyelids, and skin. The hyoid bone is fractured. There is significant vaginal bruising present, consistent with forcible sexual activity. There are traumatic injuries to the head, face, and limbs. Semen is not present in the vaginal cavity. There is no evidence of injury to the anal cavity or the presence of semen therein. The fingernails are medium length and coated with dark red fingernail polish. The fingernails of the right fore, middle, and ring fingers are broken. The fingernails of the left hand are intact. The hair is light brown with blonde highlights. There are no scars, tattoos, or other markings present."

Hmmm, that's a bummer… and unusual. Most kids have tats, even if they're tiny.

"There is a ligature mark on the neck below the mandible approximately five-eighths of an inch wide," he continued. "Bruising indicates the presence of two knots tied in the ligature. These are spaced approximately two and one-half inches apart and are one and one-quarter inches in diameter. The ligature mark encircles the neck and bruising is significantly heavier at the front, tapering off toward the rear. The ligature was positioned so that the knots were located either side of the windpipe."

Two knots. I bet that hurt. Sadistic son of a bitch. I looked down at the bruises and shuddered.

"Time of death," Doc involuntarily looked up at the wall clock as he spoke—though why, I have no idea—and continued, "was estimated at the crime scene by this examiner to be between midnight and two o'clock on the morning of Wednesday, the seventeenth of January. The cause of death was asphyxia due to ligature strangulation. The manner of death is homicide."

Hah, no sh... I'd already figured that out for myself.

At that point, he turned off the microphone and lapsed into conversational speak. He pursed his lips, rubbed his chin, his right elbow cupped in his left hand, and stared down at the body. "This was not an accidental homicide, one of those heat of the moment things, Kate. It was premeditated, planned well in advance, I think."

"How can you know that?" I asked.

"From the ligature marks. See these two larger bruises, here and here?" He pointed to each one in turn. "As I said in my report, those were made by knots tied in the ligature. The mere presence of those knots indicates that the perp

63

prepared the ligature in advance. That shows intent and premeditation. The broken fingernails, the other injuries, indicate she fought her attacker, probably grabbed the ligature. Unfortunately, no trace evidence was recovered from under her nails that might help us pinpoint the type of ligature used, but it looks like it might have been a piece of cord or even rope."

I gazed down at her as Carol began to stitch the incisions closed. It was a pitiful sight, the more so because she had yet to be properly identified. *Maybe when I get back to the office…*

"She was raped?" I asked.

He nodded, "No doubt about it. He raped her then he strangled her. Cold-blooded son of a bitch."

"So, no semen?"

"No. He must have used a condom. I'll know for sure when I get the results of the rape kit. Drugs? Alcohol? I won't know that until I get the toxicology report. So, there you have it. Questions?"

What was there to ask? I shook my head, then, taking my iPhone from my pocket, said, "D'you mind?" I nodded toward the dead girl's face.

"Be my guest," he said, at the same time glancing at the clock. "I need to get moving. It's already well past lunchtime. You want to join me?"

That was the last thing I wanted. Love him as much as I do, I'd had enough of him for one day... When I say love, I don't mean that I *love* him. I mean... Oh hell, you know what I mean. I thanked him and turned down his lunch offer as I explained that I had things I needed to do too, which wasn't a lie. I snapped a couple pictures of the dead girl's face, and I left him. I stripped off the paper suit, climbed into my jacket, hurried out the door, and then headed home. I needed a shower, coffee, and a sandwich.

Chapter 8

After leaving the forensic center, I realized how much I was looking forward to getting home. I could have showered at the PD, but what the hell? I needed a break, even if it was just a short one, and it was. By two o'clock, I was back at work, somewhat refreshed, dressed in clean clothes, and feeling a whole lot better than I did when I left the Butcher of Amnicola... *hey, I like that. Must tell Doc. Haha.*

The first thing I did when I returned to my office was to check with Missing Persons to see if anything had come in; there was nothing, and that pissed me off big time. Was this kid so unimportant no one had noted that she wasn't around anymore?

I opened the door and stepped out. Lonnie was seated at his desk in the tiny cubicle that once had been my own. He glanced up when he heard the door open. I pointed at him and stepped back into my office. He must have gotten the message because a couple of minutes later he poked his head in the door.

"You *want* me!" He stated with a grin. There was no mistaking the double entendre.

"In your dreams," I said as I gave him a look that would have frozen the nuts off a polar bear. "Go get Frost and Tracy."

"So, who is Saffron?" I asked, as I wrote her name on the white board hanging from the wall behind my desk.

I turned and looked at my small group; just Lonnie and two other detectives. "That's job number one. We need to find out who she is." Silence.

Inwardly, I rolled my eyes. Once again Chief Johnston had excelled himself in his choices for my team. Oh, Lonnie was okay. The other two? They'd both been with me for several months, and I got along with them okay... well, with Jack Frost I did. Dick Tracy—Dick was his nickname. His real name was John—now that was another story. Johnston was not responsible for that choice—I'll explain in a minute. The man, Tracy, now had more than seventeen years' experience in Vice and almost none in Homicide. This time he'd been foisted on me by a vengeful—maybe that's not the right word—the man is an ass... an assistant chief. Anyway, Tracy and I had run a case together back in the day at the time Harry had left the force... 2008, it was, and we didn't get along, not at all. Now he was back, had been for a couple of months. He was leaning against the office wall, his arms folded, a snide smirk pulling at the corners of his mouth. *I'll fix him.*

"Detective Tracy," I said. "I'd like you and Jack to start calling the colleges and universities. Talk to the records departments, see if you can find a female by the name of Saffron registered as a student. Start local," he stared at me, quizzically. "Yes, I think she's a local kid. Then work your way out to the surrounding counties, here and in North Georgia. You find her, you let me know right away. Got it?"

He nodded, pushed himself away from the wall, the smirk still set on his face, though there was little humor in his eyes. He looked at Frost, raised his eyebrows, and twitched his head toward the door. Jack nodded, got to his feet and, together, they left, closing the door softly behind them.

"You don't like Tracy, do you?" Lonnie asked, when the door closed.

I shrugged, "What's not to like? I can take him or leave him. As long as he does his job, we'll get along. He doesn't, he's gone."

I swiveled my chair around so that I could look at the big board. It was bare now, the bleak white surface broken only by the black letters of her name, Saffron. Soon it would be an unfathomable mess of scrawls—made by several different hands—photographs and notes. Storyboards such as mine were never big enough for the flood of information and ideas that would soon inundate my office.

"You never did tell me what happened between you two..."

"And I never will," I snapped, interrupting him. "Now, if you have any ideas, this would be a good time to pass them on. If not, you can get your ass outta here and go help Tracy make calls."

"Have you heard from Mike Willis?"

I looked at my watch. It was two-thirty. A little too soon, but what the hell? I picked up the phone and dialed his extension.

"This is Lieutenant Willis. Leave a message and I'll get back to you ASAP."

"Hey, Mike. It's Kate Gazzara. Give me a call, please." And I hung up.

"Damn. Where the hell is he?"

"Playing with his... the new toy you told me about, I shouldn't wonder," Lonnie said.

He spotted the look on my face and rose hurriedly to his feet, "Later, LT. I have some calls to make." And he couldn't get out of the door fast enough.

I swung around to face the board and stared up at the name, Saffron, only I didn't see it, well I did but... My mind wandered to Doc's

69

slaughterhouse and I was transported back to stand beside the table and look down at her face... *Damn!*

Lonnie hadn't been gone more than five minutes when the door opened and, without knocking, Assistant Chief Henry "Tiny" Finkle entered and sat down in the chair in front of my desk.

Tiny? That was his nickname around the PD, but not to his face. He was a diminutive little man: just five-eight and slim, maybe a hundred and forty pounds. Nobody knew how old he was, but he must have been in his late forties; his brown hair had yet to show the first gray hair. His thin face, high cheekbones, thin nose, and beady black eyes all reminded me of a possum. He was also a bigot and a misogynist. Twice in the past year I'd come close to reporting him for harassment, but he was smart enough to make sure there were no witnesses to his advances. It was Finkle that had saddled me with Tracy. They were two of a kind.

For what seemed like an age, he just sat there, watching me, saying nothing. The longer he sat there, the more uncomfortable I became. *What the hell does he want?*

Finally, "Where's Detective Tracy?" he asked, his eyes now focused on my chest.

Involuntarily, I glanced down to see if my blouse had come unbuttoned; it hadn't, but suddenly I felt half-naked just the same.

I didn't answer. Instead I stood up and reached for my leather jacket. I slipped into it and buttoned it, then returned to my seat.

"He's making phone calls," I said. "Why? Do you need him?" I asked, hopefully.

"No, I don't need him. I was just wondering how he was doing... You don't like him, do you?"

I shrugged, "What's not to like?" I repeated my stock answer. "He does his job. That's all I ask."

I waited. He said nothing, just stared at me. I felt even more uncomfortable.

"Was there something else, Chief? If not..."

He thought for a moment, his gaze still on my chest, then said, "Yes... I was wondering if maybe I might take you out to dinner one evening?"

Oh my God... So that's what he wanted. Oh dear. This is not happening. What the hell do I say?

"Oh my, Chief. That's... that's quite unexpected. I don't... know what to say."

He smiled. I almost shuddered. He reminded me of an alligator.

"Just say yes."

Be very careful, now, Kate.

"You know," I began, thinking hard and fast, "ordinarily, I wouldn't hesitate, but I've made it a rule that I don't date members of the department..."

"That didn't stop you screwing Harry Starke," he said quietly, his head cocked to one side, his eyes narrowed. *Son of a bitch. He has me there.*

"*That,*" I said angrily, "was a long time ago, and it's exactly why I made the rule. It didn't work then, and it won't work now. So, respectfully, Sir, I must decline your kind offer."

He nodded, opened his mouth as if to say something, then changed his mind. He nodded again, rose to his feet, turned to go, hesitated, then half turned toward me and said, thoughtfully, "So you say, Lieutenant... But haven't you been dating your present partner, Sergeant Guest?" *Damn!*

"No, Sir. Not dating. I've had dinner with him a couple of times, nothing more."

He nodded, "Yes, that's what I heard." His voice dripped sarcasm. "Well, that's all I'm asking. Nothing more..."

He paused, his eyebrows raised, the unasked question obvious.

I smiled sweetly up at him. *What the hell do I say now?*

"Let me think about it."

He nodded once more, smiled, exposing two rows of gleaming white teeth, "Yes, why don't you do that? I'll expect to hear from you soon." And, with that, he left, closing the door quietly behind him.

Think about it? I don't need to think about it, you creepy little bastard. It's not happening.

But I *would* have to think about it. I had to figure out how to get out of it without losing my job.

But that was for tomorrow. Right then I had a more pressing problem. I opened my eyes, sat up, reached for my iPhone, opened the photo I'd taken of Saffron and concentrated on it. I stared at it for several minutes, lost in thought: *What the hell were you doing? That bar is no place for a nice kid like you.* How did I know she was a nice kid? Truth is, I didn't. It was just a feeling I had.

The desk phone rang. It was Mike Willis.

"You busy, Kate?"

"Not as busy as I'd like to be. What've you got?"

"I'll come by your office. That okay?" It was, and I told him so. I also asked Lonnie to join us. He came into my office, and two minutes later there was a knock at my door.

"Come in, Mike."

Mike sat down and tossed a sheaf of papers onto the desk in front of me, "Those are printouts. You'll recall we found some hairs, fibers, and flecks of a white substance?"

I nodded.

"There were no fingerprints on the poly sheet, other than those of Benny and the Bron guy. I did find fibers on the sheet, though, and you already know I found some on the body," he continued. "They're the same: mostly nylon; some are polyester. All have the same trilobal—triangular—cross section and are dyed the same color, off-white. If we can find the source…"

"Any idea what that source might be, Mike?" Lonnie asked.

He shrugged, pulled a face, then squinted thoughtfully, "I can't say for sure, but they look like carpet fibers to me… maybe a bedroom throw rug, or an area rug; something like that."

Lonnie and I nodded at the same time; Mike continued.

"The hairs we found on the body? Now they're interesting. Some are human, brown—no follicles, so no DNA, I'm afraid. Some are dog hairs. I couldn't identify the breed, so I've sent samples to the FBI crime lab at Quantico. They'll figure it out. Might be useful, right?"

I nodded, then said, "Damn! No useable hair samples, no trace evidence, and no semen, so no DNA. How about the fibers? Any chance we could run down the origin?"

"No. They could have been made anywhere, from Chattanooga to China. As I said, they'll be useful only if we can find the original source."

I sighed, shook my head, exasperated, "What about the fragments of white material?" I asked.

He grinned.

"Now those are *really* interesting. They are fragments of cigarette paper. One of them has traces of saliva on it. I've sent it to Quantico too. Maybe we'll get lucky."

"Well," I said, "that's something. If there's DNA present, and CODIS provides a match, we'll solve this case pretty damn quick."

"Er, maybe not so quick. It could be as long as three months before we get a report."

"Oh, m'God, Mike. I know they are slow, but that's ridiculous. He could kill again while we're waiting, several times."

He shrugged, "True, but that's the way of it. The FBI wheels turn mighty slowly."

I sighed again, "Okay, Mike. Is that it?"

"Yes. Sorry, Kate."

"No need to be sorry. We'll just have to wait for the FBI. Okay, if you think of anything, anything at all, give me a buzz," I said, rising from my chair. It was an easy way for me to ask him to leave. As I've said, the man is a talker.

I waited until he closed the door behind him, then I said, "So what do we have, Lonnie? A whole bunch of nothing; well, nothing we can use, not yet anyway."

"We need an ID on the girl," he replied. "Then we can talk to the people who knew her, maybe pick up some leads. Without that..."

I nodded, "What *do* we know about her?" I asked. "From what Laura told us she was well-dressed, but we don't have her clothes. We *do* know that she wasn't homeless—she was well-nourished, expensive hair treatment... I'm thinking student; possibly at one of the expensive schools: Lee, maybe, or Belle Edmondson up on Signal. Hold that thought. I'll give Tracy a buzz and have him concentrate on those two schools first."

I grabbed the handset and punched the button.

He picked up on the first ring. That made me wonder what the hell he was doing.

"Detective Tracy," he said.

"No luck yet, I take it."

"No, not yet."

"Have you called Lee University yet, or Belle Edmondson?"

"No. You said to work the local schools first. That's what I'm doing."

"Well, drop those for now, John. I want you to get going on Belle and have Jack contact Lee. Let me know if either of you find anything." I hung up, looked at Lonnie. He grinned at me. I rolled my eyes, stood, turned to face the white board, grabbed a dry-erase marker, and said, as I looked at Saffron's name, "So we know she was alive at ten o'clock when, according to Laura, she left the Sorbonne. And we know she was dead at three in the morning when T.J. found her."

I wrote TOD = between 12am & 2am

"Doc says she died between midnight and two in the morning, no earlier. So where the hell was she between ten and two? We know she left the Sorbonne with a man. Okay, so where did they go and how did they get there?"

"Laura said she thought she was waiting for him, the man. If she was a hooker..." Lonnie said.

"Nope, I'm not buying it," I said. "She might have been an escort, but there's no way she was a street walker. There are bruises on her body, so whoever did this to her, beat her, but other than that, she was... in too good a shape: clean, no signs of skin problems, and I too noticed the haircut. Laura's right; it was expensive."

"So, they must have left in a vehicle, then. Does Benny have security cameras?"

"In your dreams... well, yes. He has them inside... Whoa. That means he should have footage of her and the guy. Damn! I must be losing it. How the hell did I forget that?"

I sat down, angry as hell with myself, picked up my phone and dialed the number. It was answered on the fourth ring by a sleepy Benny Hinkle, "Yeah, whadda ya want?"

"Benny. It's Kate Gazzara. You have security footage from Tuesday night, yes?"

He was silent for a moment, then said, "Yeah, maybe, if the system was working. It was on the blink all last week. I haven't checked. You want me to?"

"Yes, that would be nice, Benny," I said, sarcastically. "I'll have a uniform drop by in, say," I looked at my watch, "twenty minutes. Have it ready please." I hung up without waiting for him to answer and was just about to call Traffic when Lonnie stood up.

"Don't bother, Kate. I'll go myself. I'll be back in thirty." He left, and, good as his word, was back in a little more than thirty-five minutes with two DVDs.

"You take one," I said. "I'll take the other."

He nodded and loaded one of the disks into his laptop. I loaded the other one into my desktop computer and fast forwarded the footage to eight-forty-five on the evening of Tuesday the seventeenth. The footage was recorded by a camera positioned over the entrance to the passageway that led to the restrooms and captured the activity taking place in most of the bar area, from the rear to the front.

She entered the bar at eight-fifty-four, walked all the way to the far end, and sat down on the stool at the point where the counter curved back toward the wall. *No, she was no hooker. Escort... maybe.*

The footage was... not good: dark and laced with snow, electrical interference. Benny was right. The system needed attention, but I pressed on, hoping it would clear. It didn't. Even so, the girl looked good. Her clothes, as Laura had observed, weren't out of the ordinary, but they weren't cheap either. The green parka must have cost a couple hundred dollars; the jeans, boots, and sweater were all quality fashions too.

She hadn't been seated more than a couple of minutes when a lanky kid rose from one of the booths and approached her. He leaned on the bar and said something.

She smiled—*oh, m'God, her face lit up. She was beautiful*—shook her head slightly, and leaned away from him. He stood up straight, tilted his head a little to one side—I couldn't see his face, but I knew from his body language that he was smiling—then he nodded and returned to his booth. It happened again some few minutes later. I noted the time stamp—nine-ten. This time it was a guy at the other end of the bar, sitting by himself, nursing a drink. He got up, walked the length of the bar, perched himself on the stool next to her, leaned in, and seemed to whisper something to her. *That guy thinks she's a hooker.*

He got the same treatment as the fellow from the booth.

Neither encounter lasted more than two minutes. She constantly checked her watch. *She's waiting for someone.*

And she was. He arrived at nine-forty-eight. At the sight of him, her face lit up again. *Oh yes, she knew him.*

He was dressed as Laura said: jeans, navy-blue puffer jacket, and a ball cap with some sort of logo on the front. The cap was pulled down over his eyes, but the footage was too dark for me to get a good look at the logo. It did, however, look familiar. He walked across the bar to join her, his hands in the jacket pockets, face low and turned toward the bar, well hidden—intentional, I was sure of it, and that meant he'd been in there before, often enough to know about the location of the cameras and the security system. *Now that's very interesting.*

She leaned close and whispered something; they both laughed. He spoke again; she laughed again and called Laura over and ordered two drinks: one for her and one for him. Then she leaned forward, put a hand on his shoulder, and whispered something in his ear.

Oh yes, she knew him, and she was having a good time. No doubt about it.

81

Throughout their interactions, and almost the entire time he was there, he continued looking down at the bar top. Not once did the camera get a good look at his face. *He's hiding his face, damn it.*

They talked a little while longer, then he reached out, grasped her hand and gave it a squeeze, stood, pulled her to her feet, and then they were gone. The tell-tale at the bottom of the footage timed their exit at ten-oh-four. They'd been together for just sixteen minutes. I looked away from the screen. Lonnie was still watching his footage.

"Anything?" I asked.

"Yes, plenty. Well, plenty of her, but nothing else. The quality is terrible. How about you?"

"The same," I said as I ejected the disk and flipped it to Lonnie, "Here, see what you can make of it."

I inserted the second disk into my computer and loaded the footage. Lonnie was right, the quality was so bad it was barely viewable. It was shot from a position above the booths opposite the bar. It would have provided a good look at both of them, had it not been for the snow on the screen. Even so, I could see that the guy managed to keep his face well hidden from that camera too.

I sighed, ejected the disk, and slipped it into its cover. It was at that moment there was a knock at the door.

"Come in," I yelled.

Chapter 9

It was just after four that afternoon when John Tracy knocked at my door and stuck his head inside my office. I was instantly filled with hope. The security footage from the Sorbonne had given us little, except a verification of Laura's description of the guy Saffron had obviously been waiting for, and confirmation of my own thought that she, Saffron, wasn't a hooker, at least not a street walker.

"You got a minute, LT.?" he asked. "I think I've found her."

"Sit down, John. What have you got?"

"If it is her, her name is Saffron Brooks. She was a communications major, a senior, at Belle Edmondson. I talked to some woman in admin...," he glanced down at his iPad, "Locke, her name was. She recognized the name, Saffron. It's unusual, I guess. Anyway, she didn't know anything. She said she'd make some calls, see if she could find Saffron and have her call me. Well, she just called back, the Locke woman did, and said she couldn't find her, and that as far as she could tell, Saffron wasn't on campus, and that's all she knew. It's her, LT., has to be."

I stood, "Go and tell Frost to drop everything. We're heading up to the school.

Lonnie, go get the car. Belle Edmondson is outside the city's jurisdiction, so I need to call the Sheriff and let him know we're heading up there."

They left and I made the call. Sheriff Lucas "Whitey" White said he'd have a deputy meet us there. *Now there's a good cop, Whitey, and cute. If he wasn't married... Hah, that's funny! Belle Edmondson... Oh my. That brings back memories.*

Some years ago, Chief Johnston's daughter Emily went missing, and it was Harry Starke the chief turned to for help finding her. Emily was a student at Belle Edmondson, but that's a tale for another day, one I'll never forget. Now, I'm heading back up there, and I hope we're wrong.

Belle Edmondson College was a once glorious place, a pre-Civil War military academy. Today, it's an exclusive, and very expensive, college for women. Deputy Simpson was waiting in his cruiser parked by the massive, ornate iron gates, a relic of a once-grand era. *And they're still in need of a coat of paint,* I thought, as Lonnie pulled up beside the deputy's cruiser.

"You wanna follow us?" Lonnie yelled through the open windows. Simpson pointed forward with a gloved hand, and pulled away through the gates and onto the winding driveway.

Thinks he's in the cavalry, I mused.

We parked in the gravel semicircle in front of the administration building, a three-story crenellated edifice that also belonged to an era long in the past, surrounded by vast stretches of manicured lawns and flanked by ten three-story buildings, all of them constructed using tan-colored limestone: the halls where the ladies learned how to be ladies, among other things, all useless to anybody but the wealthy.

We left Deputy Simpson in his cruiser and mounted the flight of stone steps at the front of the administration building. Just as it was the first time I visited, the place was deserted; our footsteps echoed around the vast lobby. Well, it was, after all, nearly six o'clock in the evening.

I tapped the plunger of the old-fashioned bell on the counter top and waited. I hit it again, three times, and was rewarded by the appearance of a diminutive little woman with a worried look on her face.

"Detective Tracy?" The woman looked at Lonnie, who shook his head.

"I'm Tracy," John said, "You must be Ms. Locke. This is Lieutenant Gazzara, Sergeant Guest, and Detective Frost."

She nodded, absently, her mind obviously on other more pressing things.

"I made a list of Saffron's friends," Locke said, handing Tracy a sheet of paper. He passed it to me. "It's not a long list, as you can see. She was something of a loner. Be that as it may, I've contacted all of them and told them to expect you. You'll see that I've listed their building and room numbers. I hope I'm doing the right thing. After all, it may not be her, your... well, it may not be her," she repeated. "Anyway, I've also listed her personal details for you... well, just her name, cell number, home address, parents' names, that sort of thing... I did try to call her, by the way, but the call went straight to voicemail so I left a message for her to call me. Now, I must return to work. If you need me, I'll be here for another hour. Then I have to go home. Is there anything else I can do for you at this point?"

"No, thank you," I said. "If I need you, I'll let you know."

We left her and headed back out into the waning light. It was now after six, growing dark, and turning colder. We were, after all, on top of Signal Mountain in the middle of a very cold winter.

I gathered my team in the lobby and looked at the list of names. Locke was right; it was a very short list, just three names. *Strange!* I thought. *She was a senior in a college for women and she only had three friends. Hmmm.*

87

Jennifer "J.J." James was listed as Saffron's roommate and closest friend. The other two girls on the list were Heather Colson and Georgia Hofstadter.

I would interview the BFF, J.J. James. Colson and Hofstadter were roommates, so I had Tracy and Frost talk to them; Lonnie, I had stay with me.

For once, things went according to plan. All of the girls were in their rooms. *Thank heaven for small miracles.*

I knocked on James's door and didn't have long to wait. It was opened almost immediately by a worried-looking young woman dressed in jeans and a t-shirt.

"Hello," she said. "I've been expecting you." Her accent was pure Boston.

I offered her my ID and told her who I was and that I wanted to talk to her about Saffron.

She nodded, stepped back, opened the door wider, and asked us in.

"Please, sit down," she said as she waved a hand at the sofa set against the wall under the window. "You've... you've found her?" she asked, her voice quavering.

"I don't know. Maybe you can help."

I showed her the photo on my iPhone.

She took the phone from me and held it in both hands, pulled it closer to her, and looked down at it.

"Oh my God," she gasped, and sat down abruptly on the bed, tears already streaming down her cheeks.

She looked up at me, "It's her... What happened... t-t-to... her?"

I took the phone from her, closed the photo, and turned on my recorder.

"I'm sorry, Jennifer," I said. "I can't imagine what you must be feeling, but I need to ask you some questions and I'll be recording our conversation. Is that all right with you?"

She nodded.

"I need for you to say it out loud for the record, please, Jennifer." She did, and I added the time and date, also noting the names of all who were present.

"Please," she said when I'd finished. "I have to know. What happened to her?"

"I'm sorry. I can't tell you. We don't know..."

"But you know how she died," she interrupted me.

I shook my head, "I'm sorry, Jennifer. I'm not at liberty to discuss any of the details."

She stared at me, blinked rapidly, and sobbed, crying openly.

"When did you last see her?" I asked gently.

"On Tuesday evening. We ate here, in our room. We do... did that quite often. She said she was going out to meet someone. She didn't say who. She left at about eight saying she'd be back around eleven, but that I wasn't to wait up for her."

"Weren't you concerned when she didn't return?"

She shook her head, "No. She often stayed out all night."

"But the following morning; she had classes..."

"No. It was an out-study day, for both of us. We're majoring in Communication Arts. The school has an arrangement with several of the local radio and TV stations. I assumed that's where she was, at one of them."

"What was she driving?" I asked.

"She has... had a Honda CRV, a new one, black. Her parents bought it for her. It was a Christmas present."

"How about the license number?" I asked, not really expecting her to know it. I was right, she shook her head and stared down at her hands clasped together in her lap.

"How about friends?" I asked. "Boyfriends?"

She looked up at me and shook her head. Her eyes were red and puffy, her face streaked with tears.

"No, no boyfriends, not permanent ones, that I know of."

"That's a strange answer, Jennifer. What exactly d'you mean?"

"Well, she was kind of a free spirit. She hated relationships."

"Go on. Was she... was she gay?"

"Oh no, nothing like that... She, she liked men..." Then she grimaced and said, her voice almost a whisper, "She liked variety."

"She liked variety," I repeated, then I turned and looked at Lonnie. He just shrugged.

"What the... What exactly does *that* mean?" I asked.

She gulped, looked around, grabbed a tissue from the nightstand, and wiped her eyes.

"What I said. She liked variety," she said defiantly. "She liked sex, a lot, and with different men, lots of different men. I don't think she ever saw any one of them more than a couple of times. She was attached to no one, and she always made it very clear to every man she met that she wasn't looking for a relationship, just a... a one night stand, two or three at the most."

Oh, m'God, that I was not *expecting.*

"You're telling me that she was a nympho?" I asked, incredulously. Yes, I know, I could have put it a little more delicately, but what the hell? I was in shock. Lonnie was smiling.

"No, that's not what I'm telling you. She wasn't. She just liked to try different... to experiment. I don't know why, Lieutenant. It's just the way she was... inquisitive."

Inquisitive? That's a new one. Wow!

"And you don't know the names of any of these men?" I asked.

"Hah, Jim, Jack, John... whatever. She'd come home and talk about them, but never mentioned any personal details... except for the size of..." she trailed off, embarrassed.

"Does anyone else know about her... let's say, proclivity, for want of a better word?"

"I shouldn't think so. Although she wasn't ashamed of it. She just didn't talk about it, except with me."

"Do you know who she was meeting on Tuesday evening?"

She didn't answer, just looked at me and shook her head.

I sat there for a moment, thinking, watching her, wondering if she was telling the truth. She was upset, very upset, that was for sure, but I had a feeling there was something else going on.

"How about you?" I asked. "Were you into that sort of thing?"

I watched her eyes, something I'd learned from Harry. She blinked, once, then looked away quickly. I smiled to myself.

"You want to tell me about it?"

She turned again to look at me, "There's nothing to tell, really. I did it a few times. I wasn't into it the way she was. For me, it was fun. For her... well, it was more than that, a compulsion almost. We'd go to a bar, pick up a couple of guys, and then... Well, you know. Then we'd laugh all the way home. I never did it by myself; always with her."

"Weren't you afraid you might catch something? Wasn't Saffron afraid?"

She shrugged, "We were very picky, and they had to use... well, you know."

"No, I don't know. It all sounds kinda crazy to me. Why didn't you go with her on Tuesday?"

"It was a one-off. Someone she'd met over the weekend, at the gym. She worked out a lot. Usually at Smart's—we have a nice gym here, but it was..."

"A great place to pick up guys," I finished for her.

She nodded.

"How about you?"

"No, I told you. I wasn't into it the way she was."

I sighed. There was little more I could learn from her, I was sure of it, so I told her I'd be in touch and closed out the interview.

"By the way," I said, "you wouldn't happen to have a recent photo of her, would you?"

She nodded, picked up her phone from the nightstand, tapped for a few seconds, then handed it to me. Saffron Brooks was indeed a pretty girl.

I took a liberty and forwarded it to my own phone.

"Now you have my number. Please, if you think of anything, anything at all, call me."

She nodded and I handed the phone back to her. We left her sitting on the edge of her bed, the phone clasped in both hands, staring at the photo. I said goodbye as we let ourselves out and then we went to find the others. They were waiting for us in the cruisers.

"Back to the office, Guys," I said. "We'll talk there, okay?"

I thanked Deputy Simpson, slipped into the cruiser beside Lonnie, and we all headed back down the long driveway toward the town of Signal Mountain and onward to the PD on Amnicola.

Chapter 10

"Okay," I said, briskly, once we were all gathered in my office. "The first thing we need to do is contact her parents and break the news to them. I'll do that, right now, as a matter of fact. Give me a minute alone and then come on back."

I waited until they'd all left and the door was closed, then I took a deep breath and dialed the Boston number Ms. Locke at Belle Edmondson had provided. It was answered almost immediately by Dr. Brooks, the girl's father.

There's never a good way to hand someone the bad news; it's traumatic, *sheesh, is* that *not an understatement? Devastating would be a better word, but even that wouldn't suffice, not for me anyway.*

I've done it so many times I've almost become numb to it. I have to admit, though, that the telephone is not the right way to do it; it's much better done in person... no, it isn't. There's no *good* way to do it. I much prefer to do it that way. It's quick and it's clean, usually... So, when he answered, I just told him, as gently as I possibly could, that his daughter was dead and that they needed to come and identify the body.

People react differently to such news. Some simply sob into the phone, some shout and rage, some take it on the chin, quietly and with dignity. The gasp, and then the howl of anguish, at the other end of the line left me in no doubt how the news had been received by Dr. Brooks. I might as well have whacked the man with a hammer.

It took him a few minutes to recover, and when he did he became extremely angry, he raged and roared, and I listened, not knowing what to say. He raved on for several moments, shouting questions, one after the other, not waiting for answers. I took it all without saying more than I had to. Told him more than once, several times in fact, that I couldn't answer any questions over the phone, but I'd be pleased to tell him all I knew when I could do it in person. Finally, he calmed down a little, apologized, sort of, and asked for instructions, which I supplied. He said they'd leave right away and then he hung up. I gently and thoughtfully returned the handset to its cradle and sat back in my chair. There were questions I'd needed to ask, but that wasn't the time. I sighed and shook my head. It never got any easier.

I rose to my feet, went to the door, opened it and gestured for my crew to rejoin me.

"How did it go?" Lonnie asked, as he dumped himself down in one of the chairs in front of my desk.

I gave him a look that would have turned a lesser man to stone, but he just grinned at me, raised his eyebrows and cocked his head to one side, the question still unanswered.

"How the hell d'you think it went, Lonnie? He didn't take it well, okay? Now let's get on."

I went to the white board, grabbed the black marker, and updated her name. Then, to one side of the board, I began adding a list of what we knew, or what we thought we knew:

1. Human Hairs

2. Dog Hairs

3. Nylon Fibers – Rug? Carpet?

4. Cigarette Paper

"None of that is any help until we get the results back from the FBI," I said, without looking round.

5. Sorbonne: White Male, Black Ball Cap

"Right now, he's our only lead."

6. Logo on the ball cap?

"I'll have Mike Willis see if we can get that logo enhanced."

7. Saffron Brooks: One Night Stands – Weird Sex

"This girl had a weird sex life," I said, "and a dangerous one. She was into pickups and experimentation." I looked at Tracy, then at Frost, "Colson and Hofstadter," I said, "they said nothing of that?"

"No," Frost said. "They never mentioned anything like that. Not a word."

"Hmmm. Okay. Why not? I wonder."

"Maybe they didn't know," this from Tracy.

"You think?" I asked. "I don't. According to J.J. she made no attempt to hide it. And that brings me to J.J. I added her name to the list.

8. Jennifer "J.J." James – Same, but not so much.

"They were both at it, but J.J. not as frequently as Saffron. At least that's what she told me. I think we need to talk to that girl again."

9. Smart's Gym

"We know she went there to work out, and that she met someone there. I've been to Smart's. It's a popular national chain. We need to go visit, see if anyone there knew her. Better yet, find out if anyone saw Logo Cap there, or anyone else she might have known, or arranged to meet. Those places are usually jam-packed with predators on the prowl, at least that one was when I was there," I smiled at the memory. *Good for a girl's ego.* "Maybe we'll get lucky."

10. Saffron's Car - Black Honda CRV

"Where is it?" I glanced at Frost. "Jack, make a note. When we get done here, I want you to run her name through DMV, see if we can get the registration information. John, I want you to go see Mike Willis. I've asked him to try to enhance the image of our friend Ball Cap. I've also sent him a photo of Saffron. I need him to make prints of both. Yes," I said, answering Lonnie's unasked question. "Bad as the quality is, I want the one showing the two of them together in the Sorbonne. It might trigger a memory for someone who's seen them out together somewhere. Anyway, John, go pick them up, drop copies off here, and then go visit Smart's Gym. Show the photos around. See what you can find out. Maybe somebody will recognize the guy. Okay, that's it for now. Questions, anyone?"

"That car," Lonnie said, thoughtfully stroking his chin, "the SUV that T.J. saw. He said it was a dark color. Maybe it was hers. It's possible whoever killed her used it to transport her to the dump site. And then got rid of it. We need to find that Honda."

"You're right," I said. "Jack, call Captain Peck in Traffic and ask him to be on the lookout for an abandoned CRV." I paused, thought for a minute, then looked at my watch; it was almost ten o'clock and, suddenly, I felt very tired. "It's been a long day, guys, and it's late. Everyone's gone home by now, I'm sure, so we'll leave everything until tomorrow; start afresh then. Right now, I'm tired, hungry, and I need sleep. Let's go home. We'll meet back here in the morning at... nine o'clock. Okay?"

It was, and we left.

When I arrived home, I went straight to bed, fell facedown on it, and when I woke at six-thirty the following morning I was still like that: facedown, fully dressed, my hair in my mouth, my left arm numb and tingly from the inner elbow to my fingertips, where I'd been lying on it.

I dragged myself into the bathroom, stripped, showered, brushed my teeth, tried to do something with my hair; couldn't, so I hoisted it up into a twist on top of my head. *One of these days I'm gonna have it all cut off!* Then, as I looked at myself in the mirror, I shook my head. *Nah! It just needs a little TLC is all. Maybe I can go see Camille, have it trimmed, a few highlights, maybe... Maybe, maybe, maybe. What the hell happened to Saffron after she left the Sorbonne? There's almost a five-hour gap between then and when T.J. found her. Where the hell was she? Who was she with? Why was she murdered? Where's her freaking car?*

The answer to that last question was waiting for me when I arrived at the office.

Chapter 11

They found Saffron's Honda parked in the Walmart lot on Gunbarrel Road.

When I arrived there at five after nine, Mike Willis already had the vehicle loaded onto the back of his wrecker, ready for transport to Amnicola.

"It's been wiped clean," he said. "I can tell that just by looking at the door handles. No keys. I'm thinking that maybe the interior isn't so clean. It's difficult to remove hairs from the carpet. We'll see. I'll let you know if I find anything."

I nodded, "Soon as you can, Mike. I need a break."

"You betcha," he said. Then he climbed into his SUV and followed the wrecker out of the lot. Me? I called Lonnie and told him I'd be late. Then I headed to Hardee's on East Brainerd for a gravy biscuit and a quart of coffee. Needless to say, it was well after nine-thirty when I arrived at the office, and who should be waiting for me? You guessed it! Assistant Chief, Rat Face Finkle. *Oh hell, it's going to be one of those days.*

But it wasn't. Late as I was, he was all smiles. Then I got it: he had something else on his mind—I shuddered at the thought.

"Good morning, Lieutenant," he said, smiling, if you could call a grimace a smile.

"Good morning, Chief. What can I do for you?"

"Oh-ah, just checking in to see how things are going with the Saffron Brooks case. Her parents will be here sometime this morning, to identify the body. I'll handle that... I've also scheduled a press conference for early this afternoon. You'll attend that, of course, along with the Brookses; don't worry, I'll do the talking. So, what else do you have for me?"

I shrugged, sitting down behind my desk and leaving him standing, looking out of the window.

"Traffic found the girl's car, but other than that there's nothing new. I'm waiting for Lieutenant Willis's report. Maybe he'll find something that will give us a lead."

He nodded, his back to me as he stared out over the parking lot, his hands clasped behind his back. I looked at his ass—I couldn't help it; I like a nice ass on a man; his wasn't. He didn't have one, the skin-tight uniform pants left little to the imagination. Suddenly, I had a vision of him naked and it wasn't pretty. Inwardly, I shuddered. I shook my head to rid myself of the unwanted image.

He turned, walked to the door, put his hand on the knob, paused, then looked back at me and said, "Kate, I get the feeling you don't like me. That's not good; for the department, for me... or for you. So, maybe it's time we got to know each other. I know what you said about dating within the department, but I have a function to attend tomorrow night. I'd like for you to join me... Look," he said smiling wickedly at me, "it's not widely known yet, but there's a captain's slot opening up in a couple of months. Your name has come up as a possible candidate. You want it, I can make it happen, or not." The smile was gone, replaced by a look that would have done a barracuda proud. He turned again to leave.

"I'm sorry, Chief. I can't make it to..."

"It wasn't a request, Lieutenant. I'll pick you up at your place at seven... Oh, and wear something sexy."

He turned his head, looking back in my direction, flashed his teeth at me, "I'll see you at the press conference this afternoon." Then he was gone before I could tell him to go screw himself.

I sat there for a moment, staring after him, stunned.

The son of a bitch has done it again, and there's not a damn thing I can do about it. Well, screw him. It's not happening.

I must have sat there for a good ten minutes, seething and stewing over it, wondering how to handle it, how to get myself out of it. Finally, I got a grip on myself, shook my head, and tried to get rid of the image of his grinning rat face.

Oh hell! Son of a bitch! Damn! I've had to put up with this kind of bullshit ever since I was a rookie. And I'm not the only one. Asking me for a date is one thing, having someone force themselves on me is something else. Trouble is, the crafty bastard is careful... Oh, m'God, I'll have to sort it out later... Maybe Bob... Nah, that would be too much. Still...

Despite myself, and the gnawing thought that I needed to get work, I couldn't get the nasty little SOB out of my head. So I sat there at my desk wondering what the hell I was going to do, then it hit me. I smiled to myself, picked up my iPhone, and texted him. *Chief. Thank you for the invitation to join you at your function. I'm pleased to accept and yes, please pick me up at my home at seven tomorrow evening.* Once I finished reading it through, I pressed send, then I sat back and waited, smiling as I stared at the screen.

I didn't have to wait long. Less than a minute later, the screen lit up. *That's terrific. Looking forward to it. Seven it is. Remember to wear something sexy.*

Now I was *really* smiling. I put the phone down, closed my eyes, and leaned back in my chair with a satisfied sigh. *Oh Chief, are you in for a surprise!* I picked up the phone, buzzed Lonnie, and asked him to join me.

"Hey, Kate," he said as he sat down in front of my desk. "What's up? You look pissed. Rat Face giving you a hard time? I saw him leave."

"Something like that," I replied.

"Anything I can do?"

I shook my head, "No. I can handle him... You know they found the girl's car, right?"

He nodded, "Maybe we'll catch a break."

***

The press conference at twelve-thirty that afternoon lasted no more than ten minutes. There was nothing to tell them. Finkle spewed some bullshit about how the case was *his* number one priority and that *he* wouldn't rest until the killer had been caught and convicted, then he first introduced the parents, Sonia and Dr. Peter Brooks, and then me as the IO—investigating officer—and that was it. I took a few questions, the answers to which were almost all, "I'm sorry, I can't answer that. It's part of the ongoing investigation."

As we walked out of the press room, Finkle put a hand on my shoulder and said, "I'm really looking forward to tomorrow evening, Kate."

"As am I, Chief," I said, sarcastically. He didn't seem to notice.

"Henry. Call me Henry, but only in private."

"Very well. Henry, then."

***

Lonnie and I were back in my office when Mike Willis called me at a little after two that afternoon. I put the phone on speaker and we listened to him tell us that his forensic examination of the Honda CRV had turned up three short, off-white nylon fibers and one polyester fiber on the driver's side floor mat; two short brown hairs; and a lot of long, light brown hairs, some of which were dyed blonde—highlights I supposed. Were the fibers a match to the ones discovered on the body? All I could dig out of him was that he thought so. They were microscopically consistent in construction and color. The hairs? The long ones—he'd found them all over the interior, some even in the trunk—he could say only that the comparisons were consistent with Saffron's hair, which was no surprise. I figured DNA would confirm Saffron as the owner of those hairs. The two short brown hairs... well, all he could tell me about them was that they were found on the driver's side headrest, and that they were human but virtually useless because they were missing the follicles. They were, however, microscopically consistent with those found on her body. Was the car used to transport her body to the dump site? That, he couldn't say.

I asked him to send me the report, thanked him, hung up, leaned back in my chair, and stared at Lonnie.

He was leaning forward on the seat, his elbows on his knees with his chin resting on his interlaced fingers. He stayed like that for several seconds, seemingly in contemplation, then took a deep breath and sat up.

"What are you thinking, Kate?"

"I'm thinking we're screwed..."

No, I was thinking *I* was screwed. To tell the truth, I hadn't expected much from the Honda. The status, then, was unchanged. No, it was Finkle I had on my mind.

"We need to find her keys, Lonnie." I stood and added the keys to the list.

11. No Keys

"We find her keys," I said, quietly, more to myself than Lonnie, "we find her killer."

Chapter 12

Assistant Chief Finkle was as good as his word. He arrived right on time and pressed my front doorbell—I had, still have—one of those video doorbells, so I knew it was him. I tapped the screen on my phone and told him I wouldn't be but a minute, then I went into the bathroom, looked in the mirror, made last minute adjustments to my hair and clothing, and then went down and opened the door.

"Good evening, Chief... Oh, are those for me?" He was holding a bouquet of white roses.

He didn't answer, well, not at first. Instead, he stood, his mouth half open, staring at me.

"What the hell? You're in... *uniform*!"

I smiled sweetly, looking down at him— even in uniform dress shoes I had nearly four inches on him—and said, "You said we were going to a function, and that it wasn't a request. Therefore, I assumed it to be an order, to attend an *official* police function with you. I thought my dress uniform would be required."

"The hell you did. I'm taking you to dinner. Go and change into..."

"Oh, wow. I'm so sorry, but that sounds like a date, and as I told you before, I don't date

111

members of the department. For one thing, it's against department policy and..." I stared him in the eye, "Chief Johnston frowns upon it, and for another, it looks bad, doesn't it? Like I might be receiving special privileges from you, and we wouldn't want that now, would we, Chief?"

He shook his head, angrily. Oh, he was pissed, barely managing to maintain his composure.

"Damn you, Gazzara! You'll regret this, I promise you."

He threw the roses down at my feet, turned, and almost ran down the steps. I watched him slam his car door, heard the motor howl as he floored the gas pedal and roared down the street, then the squeal of the tires as he slammed the car into a tight left turn, and all the while I was smiling to myself. And then I had a moment of doubt, wondered if maybe I'd gone too far... *NAH!*

I picked up the bouquet of roses, *hmmm, nice. Pity they didn't come from someone I... Oh well,* I thought, as I pressed the pedal to open the trash bin and then dumped them inside. *Good riddance. Maybe one day my prince will come.* And then I had a flashback, memories of times long gone. *Damn you, Harry Starke!*

One thing I was sure of: life for me within the department would never be the same. Assistant Chief Henry "Tiny" Finkle would see to that.

Okay, I thought. *Knowing that, how are you going to handle it? Reactive or proactive?*

That, I was sure, was going to take some figuring out. The man was a vindictive SOB, but he was also careful, and with the *Me Too* movement still grabbing daily headlines, he was sure to be even more so.

Hmmm. I guess I'll have to wait and see.

Chapter 13

The next four weeks were pure drudgery. By the end of the second week in February, the reports from the FBI, despite calls from both me and Mike Willis, still had not arrived. Day after day, endless phone calls, miles of legwork, questions, questions, questions, and all for nothing. We must have talked to a hundred people and shown them the photograph of Saffron Brooks. For a girl who put herself about, and seemingly got a kick out of getting around like J.J. James claimed she did, she was little more than a shadow. Oh, there were people who recognized her—at Smart's Gym, the Sorbonne, and several other bars and haunts of ill repute—but the memories of the girl were fleeting at best; we had *nothing*. And, on top of all that, I had several other cases to work, most of them simple, but distractions nonetheless.

The good thing though, was that I saw little of Assistant Chief Finkle. He'd stop by the office once in a while to check on the progress of the Saffron Brooks case and a couple of others I was working, and he was respectful toward me, but cold, said very little and, for the most part, left me alone. No, I wasn't fooled. I knew he hadn't dropped it and felt in my bones something big was coming. I just didn't know when or how. And somehow, he always managed to stop by Tracy's desk. What they talked about... Hell, who knew?

It was mid-morning on the Wednesday a little more than four weeks after Saffron's body had been found that things took a turn for the worse: some kids out in the county, outside my jurisdiction, were riding their bikes through a wooded area when they spotted something 'shiny' a few yards off the road in the long grass. It was... yes, you guessed it, the body of a naked woman.

It was unusual that I would be called out into the county, and I wouldn't have been had Doc Sheddon not been called out first. He immediately spotted the similarity in the ligature marks around the woman's neck. He mentioned it to the Hamilton County sheriff, Whitey White, and filled him in on the Saffron Brooks case. White didn't need a lot of filling in, though; he remembered talking to me about it when I made the courtesy call for my visit to Belle Edmondson. The call to me came from Whitey himself.

"Hello, Lieutenant," he said when I picked up the phone. "I think you might like to take a look at a body some kids found out on Randolph Road. Doc Sheddon is still out here, but he's getting ready to wrap things up and have it moved. He says it ties in with your Brooks case. I can have him wait if you won't be long."

"Oh yes, please. I'd appreciate it, and thanks for the heads-up. I appreciate it," I said, leaping out of my chair. "What's the exact address?"

I was still talking to him as I ran out the door into the incident room, excitedly waving at Lonnie to join me.

"Don't thank me yet," he said, with a chuckle. "Detectives Flowers and Akers are already on-site. It's their case. They were not pleased when I told them I was giving you the nod."

"No problem. I can handle them; they're a couple of old sweeties, especially Ron. Tell them I'll be there in twenty. Just keep the pot boiling and the body on-site until I arrive."

"Old sweeties, my ass. They're a couple of throwbacks to the time when detectives wore fedoras, smoked three packs a day, and did their interrogations with the aid of a bright light and a sap. They don't like women cops and they don't like city cops either, and you're both. Good luck, Kate."

By the time I'd finished the conversation, Lonnie already had the cruiser moving out of the lot. I gestured which direction for him to turn, thanked Whitey, and hung up.

I'd met Detectives Ron Akers and Gene Flowers several times in the past. They were indeed a couple of crusty old guys just a few months from retirement; old-school detectives, both of them—the last of the summer wine, so to speak.

Whitey was right, they weren't pleased to see us... well, Flowers definitely wasn't anyway. Akers? Eh, I always thought he had a thing for me. Anyway, they were both courteous enough. "Hey, Ron, Gene," I said, offering my hand. "It's been a while. How are things?" We shook hands all round and so got the small talk out of the way quickly. I turned to Doc Sheddon who was standing outside the taped perimeter, hands in his pockets, his big black bag on the floor beside him, staring off into the blue at something I couldn't see, and maybe he couldn't either.

"Hey you," I said.

He turned toward me, smiled, then said, "Another one, Kate, and I fear there may be more. Take a look at the ligature marks. Better wear booties. The site is two weeks old; the rain and wind have wiped it and the body clean, but you never know."

I nodded and flipped open his bag, grabbed a pair of blue booties and tossed them to Lonnie, then grabbed a pair for myself, put them on, and ducked under the tape. Doc, Lonnie, and the two county detectives followed me.

She was lying faceup, her legs spread slightly, her arms outstretched, blonde hair matted and muddy, head turned slightly to the right, eyes... well, you don't want to know.

"How long has she been here?" I asked.

"A couple of weeks at least. She's... well, you can see for yourself. There's not much left to look at. She's a stinkie."

It was Detective Akers who answered. I looked at him, not believing what I was hearing.

"A stinkie? That's a new one."

He shrugged, smiling. I looked at Doc, my eyebrows raised, questioning. He nodded.

"As you can see," he said dryly, looking at the two now smiling detectives, "and as Detective Akers so succinctly indicated, the body is in the advanced stages of decomposition," he said, staring down at the body over his half-glasses. "Can't say for sure, but it looks like she's been dead, and lying out here, for quite a while. How long is anyone's guess. I'll put a call in to UTK and have them send us a forensic entomologist. He or she should be able to narrow the TOD down considerably. Kate," he looked at me as he said it, "check out the ligature marks."

I crouched down beside the body. It was easy to spot the similarities: the angle of the contusions and the two larger bruises made by the knots in the ligature.

I stood, looked down at her, and shook my head. From what I could see, I figured she was in her early thirties, but apart from that... well, nothing. Her hair was a mess. The skull had been almost picked clean. Her teeth were in good condition, but there was nothing left in her eye sockets. There was no clothing present, nothing to indicate lifestyle or social status. She could have been one of Chattanooga's upper class or, just as easily, a member of the homeless population, or even a hooker. Without an ID it was impossible to say... *unless.*

I crouched down again, gently lifted her hand, and looked at her fingernails. They were nicely manicured and obviously well cared for; her toenails the same.

"Well, this woman looked after herself, so I don't think she was homeless. That's something."

I stood and backed up a couple of steps.

"Thanks for the heads-up, Doc," I said, then turned to the two detectives, "and to you guys, too. Thanks for letting me in. Look, we should probably get together, cooperate, help each other. I know Doc won't commit himself, not yet, but I'm certain that whoever killed this woman also killed Saffron Brooks. That was a month ago. If Doc is right about the TOD, this one was killed two weeks later. You up for it?"

Akers looked questioningly at Flowers. For a long minute, Flowers stared stoically down at the body, then nodded slowly. He looked up at me, his head tilted to one side, squinting in the watery sunlight.

"Yeah, we can do that," he said. He looked first at Akers, then again at me, and finally at Doc Sheddon, "You sure it's the same killer?"

Doc shrugged, but said nothing.

"How about you, Kate? What d'you think?"

"Yes," I said. "I'm sure of it. The ligature marks are, as far as I can see, identical to those on Saffron Brooks. Okay then. We have a deal. I'll send a copy of the Brooks file to you, and you'll let me have whatever you find. Doc, I'll need a copy of the autopsy report, please. We need to get back. Here's my card," I said as I handed it to Akers. "Call me, anytime."

Akers grinned, "Anytime?"

"Anytime," I repeated, dryly.

"Later, Doc?" I asked.

He nodded, then turned and went to join the paramedics who'd just arrived to transport the body. Lonnie and I said our goodbyes and left.

We made the drive back to the station almost in silence, which wasn't like Lonnie: something was wrong.

"Talk to me, Lonnie," I said as he turned off Highway 58 onto 153.

"About what?"

"Why the silent treatment?"

"Not silent. I was thinking."

"About what?"

He was quiet for a moment, opened his mouth to speak, hesitated, then took a deep breath and said, "I've had it, Kate. I'm going to quit, turn in my notice. I have some vacation time coming to me. I'll take that and leave at the end of the week."

I was stunned, "Bullshit," I said. "You can't be serious."

"Oh yeah. I'm serious, Kate. Friday, I'm out of it, for good."

I stared at him, my mouth hanging open. He just gripped the wheel and stared straight ahead, his eyes half-closed and a tight smile on his lips.

I shook my head, sat back in my seat, and watched the road as it slid by.

"What the hell has brought this on?" I asked, without looking at him. I don't know why, but I was suddenly very angry... No, I was pissed off, really pissed off.

"It's been coming for a while," he said. "I just can't do it anymore. Today, that girl..." He twisted his hand on the wheel, the plastic squeaking under his fingers. "She's my last one. I've seen too many. No more!"

"Oh, come *on*, Lonnie. It's what we do..."

"No, from now on it's what *you* do. Me? Not anymore. I'm almost forty-two years old and I've seen enough death and heartache to last me the rest of my life. Don't make this any more difficult for me than it already is, okay, Kate?"

I sat pondering the bombshell he'd just dropped on me.

"What will you do?" I asked, finally.

"Hah, you'll laugh if I tell you."

"Try me."

"I'm going to go to barber school, learn how to cut hair. Then I'm going to open a little shop. I should do okay. I have a lot of friends in the department who need their hair cut: a ready-made pool of customers."

I turned to look at him, "You've got to be kidding."

"Nope."

"What about me, you ass? You can't just up and leave me, just like that."

He turned and looked at me, smiling, "You'll be fine. Heck, Kate, you don't need me. You never did. You don't need anyone. You'll survive. You always do."

"Damn you, Lonnie Guest." He was wrong, of course. I depended upon him more than he could ever know.

I tried to talk him out of it, to make him change his mind, but he would have none of it. The minute we entered the PD he went straight through to HR and pulled the pin. And that's when my problems really began, but I'll get into that later.

When I got back to my office, I had Tracy and Frost perform a search of the databases: NCIC; VICAP; and UCR, the FBI's Uniform Crime Reporting database, to name a few of the better-known ones. I also had them contact the TBI, Tennessee Bureau of Investigation. My thought was twofold: One, if our perp had already killed twice using the same MO, unfortunately chances were good that there were more. If so, someone, somewhere, would know and would have added it to one or more of the national databases. Second, At that point, I was pretty sure our killer lived locally—two killings in as many weeks? That's not a crime of opportunity: not just someone passing through.

It turned out I was right.

Chapter 14

The following morning, I arrived at the PD bright and early, well, at eight-fifteen, which was early for me, to good news and bad news... No, it was bad news and terrible news. I'll give you the bad first.

The database searches had turned up two more bodies. One in Bradley County less than thirty miles away, and another in Marion County just to the west.

The body of a Cleveland, TN, woman, Sheila Pew, had been found fifteen months ago in a field off Candies Creek Ridge Road. The field, if you can call it that—actually a patch of wasteland—was protected by a steel, barred gate, only it wasn't. The gate should have been chained and locked, but if it ever had been, the chain and lock were long gone. She was found, naked, just inside the field by a resident of a nearby trailer park. She'd been dead more than a week, but the ligature marks could be seen clearly in the photographs of the body. Unfortunately, she'd been cremated by the family. The theory was that she'd been killed elsewhere and then dumped. No trace evidence had been recovered. The only similarity was the double knotted ligature, and that was enough for me. But there was more.

Eight months later, Cindy Clarke's naked body, complete with the signature ligature marks, along with nylon fibers, as well as dog and human hairs, had been found on the edge of a wooded area off Aetna Mountain Road in Marion County. This time they'd gotten to her quickly. She'd been killed on Tuesday evening, July 25, 2017, and found early the following morning. This time, there was an added bonus: it had rained the day before, leaving the ground soft, and they'd found tire impressions in the mud. Did they belong to the killer's vehicle? Good question, but unless we found the killer, we'd never know.

What we did know, from casts of the impressions made using dental plaster, was that the tires were seventeen-inch Graystoke Weather King All Season, a once popular, inexpensive import from China, and that at least two of them appeared to be fairly new with little tread wear. The tires did, however, bear some unique accidental characteristics that could help to identify them, should we ever find the vehicle.

Accidental characteristic is just a fancy term for road wear. In this instance, the casting revealed several deep cuts in the tread of one tire and a small rock embedded in one of the sipes—sipes are those small hook-shaped grooves in a tire's tread block (the part that actually touches the road) that create additional tread surface area for increased grip in wet, icy, and snowy conditions. All tires, once they've been on the road, are like fingerprints. Natural wear and tear makes each tire unique, no two are identical. Yes, what we had was a long shot, but it was something.

So, now we had four dead girls spread over fifteen months and four different, autonomous jurisdictions. Fortunately, from past experience, the police departments involved all got along and cooperated with one another fairly well. I, being the detective that had linked all four murders, was designated to lead the investigation. Sounds grand, right? It wasn't, because what it really meant was that because we working with so many agencies, we needed a coordinator. The next weeks, maybe months, I knew, were going to be something akin to a nightmare.

So that was the bad news. Now I guess you want to hear the terrible news and the rest of the story. Well, here goes.

Lonnie, as I mentioned earlier, did indeed turn in his notice that Tuesday afternoon, and he insisted on leaving that Friday. So, when I arrived at work that Wednesday morning, Lonnie had only three days remaining on the job.

It was just after one-thirty that afternoon when Assistant Chief Henry Finkle walked into my office; of course, he didn't bother to knock; he never did.

"Good afternoon, Lieutenant. How are things?" he asked brightly, dumping himself down into one of the two seats in front of my desk.

I told him all was fine, and I filled him in on the overnight developments. The funny thing was, I had the distinct impression that he wasn't listening to me. Well, whatever, he let me finish my litany, then nodded, and leaned back in his chair.

"Good, good," he said. Then he thought for a minute, worked his nose with the forefinger of his right hand, stared down and inspected it, and proceeded to wipe it on the seat cover beside him. He looked up at me and said, "I can't help but think that maybe you and I... Well, that we got off to a bad beginning, a misunderstanding, perhaps."

I stared at him without speaking.

"You know," he continued, easily, "the other day, when I came to pick you up and you were in uniform." He laughed, as if he now found it to be a huge joke. "That was a good one, Kate." And then his look and tone turned deadly serious. "Did you really misunderstand, or were you winding me up? Because if you were... well, let's just say that I meant what I said."

"What was it you said, Chief?" I asked, picking up my iPhone.

"Put the phone down, Lieutenant."

I did as I was told, and he reached over and picked it up. He looked at the screen, then tapped it to turn off the recording app.

"Pathetic," he said, returning the phone to my desk. "You must think I'm an idiot." He smiled nastily and then continued, "And speaking of idiots. Since Sergeant Guest will be leaving us on Friday, you'll be needing a new partner. Detective Tra…"

"Not a chance in hell," I interrupted him. "In fact, I want him off my case, and out of my life, *now*. He was dumped on me nearly a decade ago and it was a disaster. I'm not going through that again. If you insist, I'll go over your head."

The malevolent look he fixed on me almost made me shudder. I know I blanched… I know because I saw his mouth twitch into a tight smirk, just for a second, before it quickly disappeared.

"As of Monday," he said, so quietly I could barely hear him, "Detective Tracy *will* be your new partner. Go to Johnston, if you must. If you think he'll back you, you're mistaken. If I could fire you, Lieutenant, I would. As it is, if you refuse to work with Tracy, I'll take you off the case and assign you to Burglary. Your choice, bitch." Then he stood and looked down at me, contempt twisting his lips.

I also stood, stepped around my desk and over to the door, opened it, and then stood aside so that he could leave.

He nodded and sneered, his lips pulled tight, and then he pushed against me, face-to-face, on his way out of the door. As he did so, he raised his left hand and brushed it over my breast. He turned his head to look at me, gifted me with his shit-eating grin and said, "Nice! Very nice."

"You son of a bitch," I literally snarled at him. "You *ever* touch me again, I'll put you in the hospital for a week."

He laughed. No, he cackled like a damned hen, "You think? Better men than you, Kate; better men than you... Oh, and one more thing before I leave you. Be very careful, Kate. I'll be watching you, and when I'm not, someone else will be. The first chance I get, I'll have your pretty ass out of here; I'll have your job. If not that, I'll see that you spend the rest of your career in the basement, in Human Resources," he said, his voice little more than a whisper. Then he turned his back on me and was gone.

Oh, m'God, this can't continue. Him, and now friggin' Tracy? No! Hell no! Oh, m'God, I have to do something about Finkle.

I watched through the window as he made his way across the incident room. He stopped off at Tracy's desk on the way, spoke to him for a few seconds—they both turned and looked in my direction—then he continued on and out through the incident room door. Tracy looked at me, a sardonic grin on his face. *Life is hell,* I thought, *and then you die. Well, it ain't happening!*

I looked at my watch. It was just after two in the afternoon. *Okay, I've had enough crap for one day. I'm out of here, but first…*

I closed and locked my office door behind me, walked through the incident room, past Tracy's desk—I could feel his eyes boring into my back—and out to the corridor and into Chief Johnston's suite of offices. I stormed past the wide-eyed secretary and, without bothering to knock, I twisted the knob and pushed open the door to Johnston's office. Chattanooga PD's answer to Hulk Hogan was seated behind his desk, cell phone at his ear. He moved it from his ear to his chest.

"Do come in, Lieutenant," he said, dryly. Then into the phone, "Something's come up. I'll call you back."

He pointed to one of the two chairs in front of his desk. I sat and found myself looking up at him. *Nice one, Chief.*

He put the phone down on his desk, leaned back in his chair, clasped his hands together in front of him, and looked at me, "Well?"

"That creepy little bastard Finkle has just dropped it on me that Tracy is to be my new partner. I'm not having it, Chief. You and I, we already tried that once. It didn't work then, and I can't stand the sight of him now."

He extended his forefingers, steepled them together, put them to his pursed lips, and looked thoughtfully at me.

"Tracy is a good man. Assistant Chief Finkle told me that he needs a break."

"Tracy is a misogynist, and a bigot, and so is Finkle."

At that, he opened his eyes wide.

"*Assistant Chief* Finkle," he corrected me. "I hope you can back that accusation up, Lieutenant."

"No, I can't. The smarmy little bastard has been sexually harassing me for months, but he's careful, very careful. Tracy? It's all in his eyes and innuendo. He's constantly making smart remarks that have double meanings: sexual innuendo. He is disrespectful."

"Chief Finkle thinks highly of him."

"Yes, because they're two of a kind."

He shrugged, but didn't disagree with me.

"Tracy, he's working the Brooks case with you?"

"He is," I agreed.

He nodded, thoughtfully, "Well, I'm not about to subvert my chie…"

I stood, quickly, angrily, "In that case…"

I managed to get the first three words out before he shouted, "Sit down, Lieutenant. I was going to say that I'm not about to subvert my assistant chief, but maybe we can work something out. Now, can I finish?"

I sat and nodded. He nodded.

"You, Sergeant Guest, Tracy, and Frost have been working the Brooks case."

"Yes, but…"

"So, I want you to continue to work the case, with Tracy and Frost until you have a solution. After that, we can talk again. Now, Lieutenant, if you don't mind, I'm busy."

I stared at him. Oh, was I angry!

"*No, Sir. Not* if it means I have to accept Tracy as my partner. I'll do it, but without a partner. If not, you'll have my resignation on your desk in the morning. What's your pleasure, Chief?"

He stared at me for a long moment, his face a mask, then he nodded slowly, picked up the desk phone, punched in a couple of numbers, and waited.

"Henry? Chief Johnston. I understand you informed Detective Tracy that he would be partnering with Lieutenant Gazzara. I wish you'd consulted me first. I have a job for him myself. Please have him report to me first thing tomorrow morning." And, without waiting for an answer, he dropped the handset back in its cradle.

He leaned back in his chair and stared at me, "Satisfied?" he asked.

I nodded, feeling decidedly uncomfortable.

"I sure as hell hope so, Lieutenant, because to accommodate you I've had to piss off Henry Finkle and I now have to reassign one of my staff to make a spot for Tracy. Now, a word of warning, Kate." *Kate? Now from him, that's a first.*

The look on his face was fearsome.

"Don't ever threaten me again. No one but you could have gotten away with what you just did, but you just played *all* of your cards. If it was a bluff, good for you. If it wasn't... Well, you're the best detective in the department and I don't want to lose you. But let me repeat: don't *ever* try it again. Now get the hell out of here and find me a killer."

***

When I left the chief's office that afternoon I was in no mood to return to my office, or to deal with the inevitable animus from Tracy, and probably Finkle too.

I also knew that the next meeting between me and the assistant chief would not be pleasant. The problem was, I didn't quite know how I was going to deal with the slimy little bastard. Oh, I wasn't afraid of him, nor did I intend to take any crap from him, but I also knew that I couldn't allow the situation to continue. I either had to put a stop to it, or I had to go.

With those thoughts rattling around in my brain, I went to the lot and slid into my unmarked cruiser, then turned on the engine and just sat there, thinking. *What the hell am I going to do?*

I was exhausted. All I wanted to do that evening was take a shower and curl up in bed with a good book. The shower was easy enough. The book? Not so much. I just couldn't concentrate, mainly because I had Finkle on my mind.

One thing I knew for certain was that the situation was intolerable. I knew him well enough to know that he was going to make life difficult for me, if not near impossible. It couldn't be allowed to continue. Either he had to go or I did, and I didn't plan on it being me. But how to handle it; that was the problem.

For more than an hour, I lay there, staring up at the ceiling, my brain in a whirl. *It has to be something special, something that will get his attention...* The next thing I knew the alarm was buzzing like an angry hornet. It was time to get up and face the day.

Chapter 15

It was just after eight-thirty when I arrived at my office the following morning. Of Assistant Chief Finkle, there was no sign, and for that I was truly grateful and relieved; both for that and for the notable lack of Detective Tracy, which also was good. What was not so good was that my team had been reduced by two-thirds: Lonnie didn't make an appearance that day or the next. In fact, I didn't see him again until the following Friday evening when we, that is most of his close friends, including Harry Starke and several members of his staff, met at the Big River Grill to provide Lonnie with the send-off we all felt he deserved.

So, on my way through the situation room I tapped Detective Frost on the shoulder and asked him to join me in my office.

"So," I said, after we both were seated, "let's clear the air. Detective Tracy has been reassigned and Sergeant Guest has left us. It's just you and me, for now at least. Any questions, comments?"

Jack Frost is a good-looking kid… ah, when I say kid… Well, what I mean is he was maybe six years out of the academy—eleven years younger than me—and still full of youthful enthusiasm, for life and the job. He's tall, wears his brown hair cut short at the sides and long on top, has the most stunning blue eyes, and one of those square chins that look so good with a stubble beard, which he has.

"So, what's happened to Dick?" he asked.

"He's been reassigned. That's all you need to know, but with him and Lonnie gone we're shorthanded and I don't know when, or even if, we'll get replacements."

I must have had a psychic moment, because right then, there was a knock at the door. It opened a crack, "Lieutenant Gazzara?"

"Yes. Come in. What can I do for you?"

The door opened further and a young, uniformed officer with the most gorgeous red hair stepped inside.

"I'm Officer Janet Toliver. Chief Johnston told me to report to you... I think I'm supposed to work with you."

I stared up at her. It was the first I'd heard of it. I nodded, "That's what he said, that you're to work with me?" I asked.

She nodded.

"Okay. Janet, you said?"

She nodded again.

"If you'll give me a minute and take a seat outside, I'll give him a call and find out exactly what he has in mind."

As she closed the door behind her I picked up the phone and called Chief Johnston.

"Good morning, Lieutenant," he said, before I could speak. "I assume you're calling about your new partner."

"My what?"

"Janet. Has she not yet arrived?"

"Yes, she has but…"

"Good girl, Janet. Sorry to lose her. Treat her well; be nice to her, Kate. Teach her all you can. She's like a damned sponge; takes it all in. She's got potential, that one. That all? Good. Keep me up to speed with the investigation," and he hung up.

I slowly lowered the handset and placed it gently in its cradle.

My partner? My freaking partner? Holy cow. Who the hell is she? She looks like she's twelve years old.

"What's wrong?" Frost asked. "You look… well, you don't look so good. Are you in trouble?"

I shook my head, "No, nothing like that…" I thought for a moment, then said," I need you to give me a minute, Jack. Go back to your desk, and on your way please send Officer Toliver in. I'll give you a buzz when I'm ready."

"Well okay... If there's anything..."

"No, Jack," I interrupted him "All is good, just have her come on in. I won't be long."

He left and Officer Toliver rejoined me. I motioned to the seat that Frost had just vacated and she sat down, clasped her hands together in her lap, and gazed, wide-eyed, at me. I watched her for a second or two without speaking. She was nervous, I could tell, but other than that, except for her obvious youth, she looked entirely professional. Her red hair was tied back in a short ponytail. She was slim, trim, attractive, freckled faced, and obviously uncomfortable.

"Lieutenant Gazzara..."

"It's okay," I said, cutting her off. "Did Chief Johnston mention why he was sending you to me?"

"Just that I would be working with you. Nothing more than that. I..."

"He didn't tell you in what capacity?"

"No." She shook her head.

"Tell me a little about yourself, Janet," I said, quietly.

She took a deep breath, her eyes opened wider, something I wouldn't have believed possible, and she began.

"Well, I'm twenty-three, single..."

"No, no, no," I interrupted her. "Tell me about your education, your professional experience. The rest, the personal stuff, will keep for later."

It turned out that she had a bachelor's degree in criminal justice from UTC—the University of Tennessee at Chattanooga. *Sheesh, don't they all? Oh well, it could be worse, I suppose.*

As to her work experience, she'd graduated the academy in 2016 and spent the next eighteen months in Chief Johnston's office working as a glorified filing clerk.

So that's it, you old goat. That's how you're getting back at me for Tracy. Well, she'll do, at least for now. Hell, she can't be any worse than him; nobody can. One thing's for sure: I can't put her in plain clothes... Hell, I don't see why not. She's the same age I was...

I looked at her. She stared back, defiantly. I smiled at her. She sort of smiled back at me, obviously unsure of what I was thinking. Hell, I was unsure too.

"Okay, then, Janet. Now, please ask Detective Frost to rejoin us."

She left and they entered together a couple of minutes later.

"Jack Frost," I said, "meet Detective Janet Toliver. She's joining the team."

I smiled at her. She looked stunned.

"Plain clothes tomorrow morning, okay, Janet? Wear something comfortable."

She nodded. For a moment she was speechless. Then, "Dee... Detective? Are you kidding me?"

"No. Chief Johnston said you'd earned it. Congratulations, Janet."

Frost glanced at her, then at me, the question in his eyes, unasked.

"Welcome, Janet," he said, holding out his hand.

By then, I'd turned my back on the both of them.

"Did the chief tell you about the case we're working on?" I asked, my back to her as I scanned the white board.

"Umm, err, no, no, not really. Just that you're working a murder case."

I sighed, and then spent the next fifteen minutes giving her the short version, which was really short because I still knew little enough myself.

"Now, you're as wise as we are," I told her, with a smile. "So let's get to work."

Chapter 16

It wasn't until several days later that anything significant happened. We were now dealing with four murders, and I, together with Detectives Toliver and Frost—Tracy, much to my delight, was by then occupying a desk in the chief's offices—spent those seemingly endless days coordinating the investigation between the various jurisdictions. It wasn't a difficult job, but the paperwork it generated was beyond belief.

Of Assistant Chief Finkle, I saw very little. From time to time, though, he'd stop by to check on progress and hassle me about the lack of it, but on the whole, he left me alone. Janet settled in and turned out to be quite an asset. Her time with Chief Johnston had not been wasted. She was, as he'd said, a veritable sponge, and drawing on her ambition and clerical experience, she soon had the case organized, by timeline and by victim.

Lonnie? Well, he hadn't been gone but a couple of days before I began to miss him; other than that, life in the Palace had been relatively quiet.

The Akers/Flowers body found in Hamilton County had been identified as Melissa Perez, aged twenty-seven, a resident of Chattanooga. Mike Willis had done his thing with his magic lantern and had turned up a single nylon fiber along with a couple human and dog hairs, all stuck to the woman's naked back. There was now no doubt about it, all four victims were killed by the same perp: we were dealing with a serial killer, and that he—I figured it had to be a he—because of the extended timeline, wasn't a tourist; he lived locally, probably in Chattanooga, and possibly even in Dalton or Cleveland.

The toxicology reports on the Saffron Brooks case had arrived on February 26. They revealed nothing untoward other than an elevated level of alcohol in her system. The FBI reports arrived via fax two days later on February 28 and they added some interesting facets to the investigation, none of which provided any real help, or useable clues, not then anyway, not until we had a viable suspect.

The tiny fibers found on Saffron's body were from an inexpensive, off-white rug. Most of them were nylon, probably from the rug itself. A few were polyester, likely from the fringe. All were dyed the exact same color, an unusual off-white.

The Marion County Sheriff's Office supplied Mike Willis with samples of the fibers found on Cindy Clarke's body and he, using comparison microscopy, determined that while they appeared to be virtually identical in color, structure, and manufacture to those found on Saffron Brooks and Melissa Perez, he could only say that they *could* have come from a common source; "could" being the operative word; the common source being a cheap rug. Even so, he was prepared to say that the fibers, combined with the other trace evidence and the ligature impressions, were similar enough in each case to be considered solid evidence and that they did indeed come from the same source. *Wow, what a roundabout way to say almost nothing. Oh, m'God, now that I know they could have, might have, probably did, maybe did come from the same source, and that they... oh hell, all of that makes me feel a whole lot better... Not!*

The FBI report also confirmed that the fragments of white material found on Saffron's body were cigarette paper, brand unknown, possibly filtered but that too was uncertain. *Oh, m'God, more uncertainty.*

They also confirmed there were minute traces of saliva on the paper; minute, but still enough to get a DNA profile. They'd run the profile through CODIS, but didn't find a match. So once again, without something to compare it with, it was useless.

Again, Mike compared the tiny fragments of paper found on Cindy Clarke with those found on

Saffron, and again he managed to come up with the same conclusions. The cigarette paper was similar in construction, but he couldn't say it was identical. Again, saliva was present, and it was sent away for DNA profiling. Chief Johnston pulled strings at the lab and was promised a report within the week. It actually took ten days, and that was considered something of a record. Was it a match for that found on Saffron Brooks's body? No, it wasn't.

The FBI report also identified the hairs found on Saffron's body, all brown in color, as a mixture of human and dog hairs—the dog breed was determined to be a chocolate dachshund. *A freaking wiener dog. Oh, m'God, what next?*

And once again, Mike was only able to conclude that, without follicles, the hairs—both human and dog—were similar enough to have come from the same person and dog, but he couldn't say conclusively that they had.

All that being said, we still had almost nothing to go on. We needed a break.

I was spending more and more of my time in the office, on the telephone, coordinating what was turning into a massive investigation, talking to detectives—there were now more than two dozen from four different jurisdictions including Chattanooga, Hamilton County, Bradley County, and Marion County, plus the TBI was now involved—and we had parents, family members, friends, and acquaintances of all four girls to interview, and that information all had to be analyzed and assimilated.

I spent countless hours staring at the white board behind my desk. Slowly, over the weeks it had filled with photographs, notes, and above all, unanswered questions. Now, with the FBI and Mike Willis's reports in hand, I began to add even more information to the already overcrowded board beside the names of the four victims.

1, Saffron Brooks

2, Melissa Perez

3, Sheila Pew

4, Cindy Clarke

5, #5?

Yes, number five. No, she hadn't turned up yet, but I was certain that she was walking around out there somewhere, happily unaware of her impending doom. I was also certain that our killer was already stalking her. If not, she was already dead and waiting to be discovered.

Suspects? Hah, I didn't have any, not a one.

Clues? Yes, but it was a meager list: a few nondescript fibers, human hairs, dog hairs, fragments of cigarette paper, a solitary set of tire impressions that may or may not have been made by the killer's vehicle, and some DNA. All of it absolutely useless unless we caught a break, and we finally did.

I had Janet and Frost call tire dealers across East Tennessee, North Georgia, and Alabama to try to find out who might have purchased a set of Graystoke Weather Kings within the last five years. Yep, that was a daunting task and somewhat of a Hail Mary, but I figured we might get lucky, and we did. We found two dealers in the tri-state area that had sold such tires. Unfortunately, one of them was now out of business. The other was Pellman's Tires & More.

BillyBob Pellman ran his used parts and tire shop just over the Georgia state line on Chickamauga Avenue in Rossville.

Frost took it upon himself to go visit Pellman's Tires & More. What he found out wasn't, at first, encouraging. The Graystoke tires, because they were a third of the price of their competitors, had been quite popular and, over the five years in question, Pellman had sold a great many of them. The problem was that the brand and the tires themselves were no longer available. Like the infamous Firestone ATX, the Graystoke, a much inferior product to the recalled ATX, had suffered similar problems: the tread was prone to

149

separation at high temperatures. That being so, after the ATX debacle, the TSA had moved quickly and the Graystoke brand was withdrawn from sale in the United States. This had an adverse effect on tire dealers that relied on the sales of the cut-price products, thus resulting in BillyBob's competitor going out of business, much to his, BillyBob's, undisguised glee.

"So, what did you find out?" I asked Frost the afternoon he returned from Rossville. He was seated across from me in front of my desk, a large brown suitcase on the floor beside him.

"I'm not sure. He sells a lot of tires, as did his competitor. The ones we're interested in haven't been available for more than three years.

"He did keep records of his sales though, right?"

"Hah! If you could call them that." He hoisted the suitcase up onto his knees, flipped the locks, lifted the lid, and turned it toward me. The thing was stuffed with receipts, big fat bundles held together by straining rubber bands, each with a slip of paper attached and a dollar amount inscribed thereon.

"These," he said, dramatically, "would you believe, are Mr. Pellman's tax records. There are several thousand receipts in here. All of them are tire sales, some Graystoke, some Bridgestone, some Yokohama...Well, you get the idea. We'll have to go through each and every one of them—"

"Not the last three years, though, right?" I interrupted.

He grinned at me, "These don't include the last three years."

"Oh hell," I said, as I waved my hand toward the door. "Take them away. You and Janet get on with it. Let me know if you find anything."

"Er..." he said, as he closed the latches on the suitcase.

"What?" I asked.

"How about some help, LT.? This lot will take days to do if it's just us two."

I sighed, nodded, and picked up the phone, "Go and get started. I'll see if Captain Peck can lend us a couple of uniforms."

I punched in Peck's extension. He could, and he did.

Chapter 17

When I arrived at the police department the following morning, Tuesday, Frost and Toliver were already waiting for me. Frost followed me into my office, dropped several small bundles of paper onto my desk, then sat down. Their search of Pellman's receipts had turned up some names, a lot of names.

"We finished late last night," he began. "It's not good. Twenty people purchased Graystoke tires during the months January through April 2015—he stopped selling them in April... Well, that's when he says he ran out of stock. He sold one hundred and seventy-two in 2014, a like number in 2013, and a whopping five hundred and four in 2012. The sales were spread over an area more than forty miles in diameter, taking in most of the tri-state area, and that doesn't include the sales Pellman's competitor made...." he paused, at a loss for words.

I stared at him across the desk, slowly shaking my head. He grimaced, shrugged, and nodded his head in agreement.

"I know what you're thinking," he said.

"Oh, do you? What am I thinking?"

"You're thinking that tracking all of them down and taking tire prints is going to be a nightmare."

"No. Not even close. I was thinking that it's not going to happen, that I don't have the budget, much less the manpower."

"So what are we going to do?" he asked.

"Well, we need a break, that's for sure." I spun my chair and stared up at a map of the city.

"I've said many times that I'm pretty certain our killer is a local boy. If he is, and if he's buying, or has purchased, cheap tires, then he's looking to save money, which means he's probably blue-collar or maybe even unemployed. And that means," I said, getting to my feet and grabbing a red marker, "that he may well live in one of these areas." I drew three circles on the map. "Well, there are more, of course, but it makes sense to begin with these three locations."

He nodded, "Yep, makes sense."

I turned again to face him, "Okay," I said. "Go get Janet and let's go through these again."

I waited until the two of them were seated and then picked a small bundle of receipts and tossed it to Frost. "Sort out all of the receipts for sales to people living in any of those three areas and let's see what turns up." I looked at my... no

153

watch dammit, then continued. "You have, what? Six or seven hundred? Okay, so between you, it shouldn't take too long. Come back when you've finished... Oh, and thanks, Jack."

"For what?" he asked as he gathered together the bundles.

"For staying late and getting it done."

"No problem."

***

It was around ten o'clock that same morning that things took a turn for the worse, with both the investigation and my relationship with Assistant Chief Finkle.

I was in my office trying to make some sense of the maze of information laid out on my white board. Never in my life had I been confronted with so much data that meant so little: names, dates, places, and questions... *Questions, questions, questions... and not one damn answer. Four bodies, all connected by one significant factor: the ligature marks. All were sexually assaulted. The killer was careful—no semen present. All were beaten. Some bits and pieces of trace and a single set of tire impressions. That's it. That's all I have....*

My office door opened at the same time my phone rang. Assistant Chief Finkle entered my

154

office and sat down. I picked up the phone, "Gazzara."

I listened to the caller with mounting dread, the more so when I saw the cold look on Finkle's face.

The call was from dispatch. The naked body of a young woman had been found on a patch of wasteland off of Lupton Drive in Hixson. Two kids, girls, out riding their electric scooters, as they did most days, had spotted something in the undergrowth that they hadn't seen before. They investigated, realized what they'd found, and called 911. The call had come in at nine-seventeen. A cruiser had been dispatched and the scene secured.

"I'm coming with you," Finkle said, rising to his feet. "You can drive."

My blood ran cold. The last thing I wanted right then was to be alone in a car with that SOB, and he could tell what I was thinking.

"I *said*, you can drive. Now get your shit together and let's go."

And, reluctantly, that's what I did.

***

Lupton City is not really a city at all; it's a quiet, mostly residential area on the north side of the Tennessee River off Hixson Pike. There are public areas—parks, tennis courts, soccer fields, and picturesque walks and... quiet roads where kids can ride their bikes in relative safety. It is, by any standards, a desirable place to settle and bring up a family; there were plenty of places where couples looking for somewhere to spend a few quiet moments alone could get out of sight and enjoy themselves. The body was found in one such place: just inside the entrance to a section of wasteland surrounded by tall shrubbery and undergrowth.

The body wasn't hidden exactly, but it was out of sight of passersby. You had to drive off the road and into the patch of wasteland to see it, which is exactly what the pair of twelve-year-olds had done, as they always did when out and about on rides: it was one of the must-visit sites on their tour of the public areas.

The drive to Hixson was, thank God, uneventful. Assistant Chief Finkle said little and, to my relief, kept his hands to himself. We arrived at the scene only moments after the appearance of Mike Willis and his crew, and just moments before Doc Sheddon.

Lupton Drive was blocked to traffic both ways by police cruisers. The entrance to the strip of wasteland had been taped off and was being guarded by two uniforms, one of which I knew quite well, Tom O'Mally.

He grinned at me as he held up the tape for me, "We gotta stop meetin' like this, Lieutenant."

I smiled back at him as I ducked under the tape, "How are you, Tom? Long time no see." As I said it, I happened to glance round and spot the angry look on Finkle's face.

"Something bothering you, Chief?" I asked over the tape.

"Not a thing, Lieutenant," he said as he ducked to pass under the tape.

I held up my hand, "Sorry, Sir. I need for you to stay outside of the crime scene perimeter until Doc Sheddon and Lieutenant Willis and his team have finished with it.

I thought for a minute that he was going to argue, but he didn't. Reluctantly, he nodded, and stepped away, his face red, but it would have been a whole lot redder had he spotted the grin on Tom O'Mally's face.

I stayed well back too, looking around the scene, waiting to be called forward. It was then that I spotted the tire impressions. I should have noticed them right away, and would have had I not been distracted by the ominous presence of Assistant Chief Finkle. Fortunately, neither I nor the two

157

girls had disturbed them and I could see that some, not all, were quite well defined: crisp and clear—it had rained the previous evening, just enough to soften the ground; we had indeed gotten lucky.

I stood in front of them, guarding them jealously, and looked around. Mike Willis, covered from head to toe in white Tyvek and carrying a tech bag, was just passing through the tapes.

I waved a hand at him and pointed to the impressions. He quickly joined me and we stood together, gazing down at them; the body, lying just a half-dozen yards away to the left, was ignored, at least for the moment.

"Oooh, those really are lovely!" Mike had put the bag down and was rubbing his hands together. "Hey, Mooney," he yelled to one of his techs, "I need you to make casts of these, quick as you can." Mooney, a lady tech I'd never met, nodded and headed back to the CSI vehicle.

"Now," Mike said, stepping back and away from the impressions, "let's take a look at the victim."

"Good day to you, Kate, Mike," Doc Sheddon said, when he stepped up beside us and joined in as we stared down at the remains of what once had been an obviously attractive young woman. "So," he said, as he crouched down beside her and placed two fingers on her neck, "another one, eh? She's not been here long either. Maybe two hours, three at the most."

"What?" I asked, as I looked at my watch. "Are you sure?" Wrong question, as was evidenced by the look Sheddon rewarded me with.

"Of course you are," I said, hurriedly, and smiled at him in a manner, that I hoped, conveyed a sincere sense of appeasement. "But that means it must have been broad daylight when she was left out here. Seven o'clock at the earliest."

He nodded, "She's been dead for several hours, but the body is still quite warm. Temp's not dropped by more than... hmmm, five or six degrees. If she'd been out here long... well, she would be a lot colder. I'll know more in just a minute." He opened his bag and first took out a digital thermometer, watched it for a few minutes, then nodded and said, "Fifty-eight degrees—nice day for it—now let's take her temp." He took a second thermometer from his bag, leaned over the body, parted her cheeks, and inserted the probe.

"Sorry about that, young lady," he said to the body. He waited, staring at his watch, timing the interval, then he removed it, stared at it, and then said, "Yep, ninety-two -point-three. Lividity is not yet completely fixed. Rigor still has a ways to go. So, depending upon where she's been kept, I'd say she died sometime between two and four o'clock this morning; closer to four than two."

I felt something touch me. I turned to find Finkle standing close behind me, too close, and suddenly I felt very uncomfortable. I would have moved, but there was nowhere to go; Doc was to my right, Mike to my left, and what remained of an obviously pretty young woman lay just feet away in front of me.

I rolled my shoulder, "Please, Chief. D'you mind stepping back a little? I can't breathe?"

He smiled, no he snarled, but did as he was asked, barely. He took half a step back, and there he remained until finally I'd had enough of him breathing down my neck and I turned and pushed past him.

Under any other circumstances I would have stayed at the scene until Doc finished his examination; not that time. I told Doc I'd call him, and Mike that I'd see him back at the PD, and then advised Finkle that I needed to get back.

"What's the hurry?" he asked, looking up at me from under the bill of his cap. His eyes were slitted, but what little I could see of them glittered. Actually, they were watering in the cold breeze, but to me they had a look of evil about them.

160

"I have things to do," I said. "We have some leads that need following up. My time is better spent doing that than hanging around here." *Especially with you!*

He nodded, "Then let's go, Lieutenant."

The ride back to the PD was a silent ordeal, for me anyway. For him? Who knows?

He made no attempt at conversation until I pulled into the lot and turned off the motor.

"Before you go, Lieutenant," he said at the same moment he put a hand on my arm; I flinched, but he didn't seem to notice. "We now have five dead girls. You tell me that you have nothing, no suspects, just a few leads. That worries me. I'm beginning to wonder if you're up to it, if I should bring in someone more qualified..."

I shrugged his hand off my arm, turned to him, and said, angrily, "You and I both know that's not going to happen. I have the full backing of Chief Johnston, and you're fully aware of that too. If this is another attempt to coerce me..."

He interrupted me, "No, absolutely not, but we can't have bodies continue to pile up this way. This thing has to be solved, closed out. The media is eating us, me, alive..."

"Well," I said, "you did tell them it was *your* case, so you can take the heat. *Please,* just let me get on with my job. Now, is that all? Can I return to my office? Are we done here?"

He was silent for a moment, staring at me, unblinking. *How does he do that?* Then finally he nodded, "Just get it done, Lieutenant."

And with that, he jerked the door handle, threw the door open, climbed out of the car, and walked stiffly into the building.

Sleep didn't come easy that night. Oh, I went to bed early enough, and I watched some silly reality show until my eyelids began to droop, then I turned the television off and settled back into the pillows as I closed my eyes, but not for long. Barely had I began to doze, when my iPhone buzzed on my nightstand.

I picked it up and tried to focus my eyes on the screen. Because I didn't recognize the number, I was just about to ignore the call, but then thought better of it and answered it.

"Hello."

"Hello, Catherine." *Catherine? No one calls me that, ever.*

The voice was husky, indistinct, as if the caller was speaking through a cloth, or something.

I sat up with a jerk. *What the hell?*

"Who is this?" I asked, demanding an answer, voice shaking with anger.

The voice laughed, huskily. He—yes, I was sure it was a he—sounded breathless.

"Oh," he gasped. "I've, I've, I've... been, watching you. Ohhhhhh, ooooooh, ahhh. Oh m'God! Thank you."

"You—filthy—Son of a Bitch. You just got off, at my expense..."

"I did, didn't I?" he asked, chuckling, and then the phone went dead. He'd disconnected.

I stared at the screen, open mouthed, the covers had fallen away when I jolted upright, leaving me naked to the waist, but I barely noticed the cold. I was stunned.

Who the hell was it? I asked myself. There was nothing about the voice I could identify, but I had a strong feeling I knew who it was: my killer.

No, sleep didn't come easy that night.

Chapter 18

The following morning when I arrived at work I headed straight for Mike Willis's office and dropped my iPhone down on the desk in front of him.

"I had a call last night," I told him. "A particularly disgusting call. The son of a bitch even called me by my full first name, *Catherine.* No one ever calls me that. Can you trace the number?"

He picked up the phone, tapped the screen a few times, then asked, "This one?" and proceeded to read off the number.

"Yes, that one."

He nodded, told me to sit down, then turned to his computer and pecked away at the keyboard for what seemed to be an interminably long time. Finally, he shook his head, sighed, turned, looked at me, and said, "The number is unregistered. It's probably a burner purchased at some off-the-wall store. I'd bet he's already tossed it. Sorry."

He handed the phone back to me. I looked at it, tapped the screen and blocked the number.

"Catherine?" he asked. I didn't even know that. I thought it was just Kate. How in God's name did *he* know it?"

"You can put that down to Assistant Chief Finkle," I said. "That's how he introduced me at the press conference. I've been called Lieutenant Catherine Gazzara by every television anchor for the past couple of months. Thanks anyway, for trying, Mike," I said, and I left him.

I stormed through the incident room, tapping Frost and Janet on the shoulder as I passed them.

"My office, now," I said, without looking round.

I unlocked the door and went to my desk, slammed my briefcase down on top of it, then turned and parked my rear on the front edge, and waited for them. They entered together.

"Janet, I never do this. I don't believe in it, but much as I hate to, I'm going to ask you to please go get me a cup of coffee, black. D'you mind?"

She didn't. In fact, she seemed pleased to do it. By the time she returned, I'd already begun to calm down, my mind moving on to other, more important things.

***

Victim number five was identified by her parents as Melody Ferber, a twenty-year-old nursing student at Chattanooga State. She lived with her parents and apparently was a fitness freak. She'd supposedly gone to Smart's Gym after she'd left school around five o'clock that Monday afternoon. *There it is again, Smart's Gym.* Unfortunately, no one had seen her there. In fact, two people, friends of Melody's, had stated categorically that she hadn't been there. So where did she go that afternoon?

Did she go on a date? If so, who with? And where did she go? The local media had run her photograph several days back to back, asking for information from anyone who might have seen Melody in a restaurant or, anywhere else, that night.

Several calls had been received and followed up on. None of them panned out. The first forty-eight hours in an investigation are crucial; we were now eight days in and we had nothing, no leads to work with. We knew no more than we did the day her body was found. The case had gone cold. Can a case go cold on eight days? Yes, and this one had; it had joined the four previous cases. Something had to give. We needed a break, and we needed it now.

The refined search of Pellman's receipts had turned up some thirty-plus likely purchases. Over the next week, they were duly tracked down and printed. It was a difficult, time-consuming process.

Mike Willis had confirmed that the impressions taken at both crime scenes were a match: they'd been made by the same vehicle. Unfortunately, none of the prints from the vehicles listed on Pellman's receipts were a match.

"Okay," I said, as I looked up at the map and drew two more circles—the area now included most of the City of Chattanooga. "Let's widen the search."

That search produced twenty-seven more likely candidates. They too were located and printed: still no match. I was at loss. I was certain the killer was local. Mike told me, and the plaster casts on my desk confirmed, that the front tires were either quite new or the vehicle in question had been driven very little; the rear tires were much more worn.

I thought long and hard about where we were and, more to the point, where we weren't. My conclusions remained unchanged: the killer was local. And so, the search for the vehicle continued.

Chapter 19

More days passed and I was still at a loss as to why we couldn't find that vehicle. I was at lunch, by myself, when it hit me. By then, I had no doubt that whoever had left those tire impressions was my killer. I was also convinced that the killer was a Chattanooga resident.

So, if the killer is a local, he bought the tires locally, which also means someone local sold them to him. Duh!

That means it was either Pellman or his out-of-business competitor... It's got to be BillyBob.

"We need to go talk to Mr. Pellman again. I'll go with you this time," I said to Frost when I arrived back at the PD later that afternoon.

"What for? You think he knows something?"

"I think he knows more than he's telling," I said.

"Janet," I said to my new partner, although she was still unaware of it, "you hold the fort while we're gone, okay? If the assistant chief drops by, you *do not* know where I am or when I'll be back. You got that? Good. If he does, drop by, find out what he wants and call me when he's gone."

I looked at my watch, "It's already after three. We may not get back to the office today. So, unless I hear from you, we'll meet here at eight in the morning. Understood?"

She nodded, "Yes. If Tiny comes by, you've gone out. I don't know where you are or when you'll be back, and I'm to find out what he wants and then call you."

I grinned at her, "Tiny?" I asked.

She smiled sheepishly, "Assistant Chief Finkle."

"That's better." We left her at her desk in the situation room.

***

BillyBob Pellman was sitting comfortably with his feet up on his desk when we arrived. His staff, all two of them, were changing the tires on a Jeep Wrangler that had seen its best days at least a dozen years earlier.

"You again," he said to Frost as we walked into his office. Then he looked at me and his eyebrows went up, his feet swung down from the desktop, and he sat upright.

"Whoa, who the hell are you?"

"Now is that any way to greet a lady?" I asked.

"Lady my ass. You're a cop, and his boss by the look of you. What is it you want this time?"

"You want to tell him?" I asked Frost, as I sat down on the single chair in front of his desk, crossed my legs, and folded my arms.

"It's about those tires, those Graystoke Weather Kings."

"What about them? I gave you all my receipts. There ain't no more."

"Ah, but did you?" I asked, raising my eyebrows.

"Yes, of course I did. Why wouldn't I?"

"And that really is the question, isn't it?" I watched his face. It was a mask of stone. "Why wouldn't you?"

"I didn't, did... I gave him all of 'em. There ain't no more. I swear."

"Oh dear," I said. "I wish you wouldn't do that."

"What? Do what?"

"Swear to something you know is a lie."

"It ain't a lie. There ain't no more."

"Look at me, Mr. Pellman." I looked him in the eye and watched for his reaction when I said, "You and I both know that you were, and probably still are, selling tires off the books, for cash, probably at a discount." And there it was, the tell. He blinked, rapidly, three times.

"I've seen the receipts you made out for the legal sales," I continued. "They are meticulously drawn up. That leads me to believe that even when you sell tires off the books, under the table so to speak, whatever, you make out receipts for those too, right? You like to keep good records."

He twitched, obviously uncomfortable. I had him, and he knew it.

"A few, maybe... not many. A little extra cash goes a long way these days."

"The receipts," I said, gently. "I want to see them. Just those for seventeen-inch Graystoke Weather King All Season tires sold in the greater Chattanooga area between January 2013 and August 2017."

He sighed, shook his head, then got up and went to a cupboard at the back of the office. He pulled out a cardboard box, returned to his desk with it and sat down again. After sorting through several dozen bundles of hand-written receipts, he finally selected three small bundles and tossed them across the desk to me.

"There. That's all of them."

I picked them up, flipped through them, and then I stripped off the paper clips and looked at each receipt in turn.

There were seventeen of them. Five sets of the tires were sold in North Alabama over a period of twenty-three months. Five more sets were sold over the same period to customers in Northwest Georgia, and seven more were sold in Hamilton County, including Chattanooga. *Seven. That's manageable.*

The receipts, though they'd been for products sold under the table for cash, were surprisingly detailed, as I guessed they would be. They contained names, dates, addresses, make and model of vehicles, and even phone numbers. Of the seven sets of Weather Kings sold in Chattanooga, all but one had been fitted to Ford Bronco IIs, an SUV that had been manufactured between 1980 and 1996. The seventh vehicle was a 2003 Chevy S-10 Blazer.

"Tell me something," I said as I waved one of the receipts at him. "You sold these to a customer less than twelve months ago. Do you have any of these tires in stock?"

He looked at me, guardedly, "They've all been recalled."

"That's not what I asked. Do you have any left in stock?"

172

He shrugged, "I might."

"Seventeen-inch?" I asked.

Again with the shrug, "Maybe."

"So how about you check and see if you do?"

"If I do, they're not in the computer. I'd have to go out and look around."

"And why would they not be in the computer?" Frost asked.

He drew in a deep breath through clenched teeth, "I told you. They've all been recalled..." he trailed off.

"And you're selling them under the table," I finished for him.

"Get your ass up and let's go," Frost growled at him.

It turned out that he did indeed have tires left in stock, four complete sets of 225/45R17.

We returned to his office and I gathered together the seventeen receipts.

"What do they sell for?" I asked.

"What? The tires?"

"Yes, you ass. The tires."

"When they were available, a hundred and eighty-five. Now, whatever I can get for them."

"Pull a set and put them somewhere safe," I said.

"Why? Wha'fore?"

"Just do it," I said tiredly. "If I need them, they'd better be here. If they're not," I waved the bunch of receipts in the air, "you know what will happen to these, right?"

He looked sadly resigned, but nodded.

I looked at my watch. It was after six.

"I've had enough for one day," I said to Frost. "Let's go home. We can start in on this lot tomorrow morning."

We left BillyBob Pellman sans receipts, sitting behind his desk sucking on a disgusting, wet, tattered old stogie, and most likely, visions of IRS agents dancing in his head. And once again I went home feeling worn out, alone, and forsaken.

Chapter 20

I slept well and woke early the following morning. I even did twenty minutes on the step climber, something I hadn't done in weeks. By the time I'd showered and eaten a couple of lightly scrambled eggs, I was feeling quite zippy and ready to face the day with a certain amount of optimism.

"What did you think of Pellman?" I asked Frost. We were in my office, me standing next to my storyboard and staring at it when I asked him for his opinion, not because I wanted to know, but for something to talk about while we waited for Janet to join us; she was unusually late that morning—she'd called in—something to do with the road conditions.

"He's a typical, sharp automotive undermarket operator, is what I think."

"Undermarket? What the hell is that?"

He grinned as he explained, "It's a word I made up for businesses that sell and/or trade cheap, used or counterfeit, aftermarket auto products. He does that. By the way, why did you want him to hold those tires for you?"

I shrugged, "No real reason. I thought maybe they might come in handy... oh hell, I don't know... Maybe I was just being ornery."

He grinned and said, "You? Ornery? Come on, LT. Not you, surely?"

"I'm sorry," Janet said as she burst through the door. "You have no idea of the traffic. There was a wreck on I-75. It was like a parking lot."

"It's okay," I said. "Sit down. We've a lot to get through."

By then, I was in the seat behind my desk, my briefcase open on top of it. I took out the small bundle of seven receipts—I left the others in the briefcase in the hopes we wouldn't need them—stripped off the paper clip and spread them out across the desktop.

"Okay," I began, "here's the deal. Janet, we recovered seventeen receipts for seventeen-inch Graystoke tires sold off the books, under the table, as it were, by Pellman's Tire Shop. Seven of them—these seven—were sold in Hamilton County, including Chattanooga. We won't bother with the others for now, instead we'll begin with just these. Maybe, just maybe, we'll get lucky."

I looked at the slips of paper, reading the names and addresses of the purchasers to myself as I did so. Three sets had been purchased by people living within the Chattanooga city limits, four out in the county. I decided to begin with the city locations. As I reviewed them, I noted particular details of each.

Michael Meeks – Hixson, Married, one teenage daughter

Roberto Hernandez – North Chattanooga, Married, two children

MaryJo Hooks – East Brainerd, Divorced, no children

"These three," I said. "They're all local. We'll begin with them. I'll see if I can get you some help."

I called Captain Peck in Traffic and begged him to lend me a couple of uniforms for a few days. He did, and I assigned one each to my two musketeers. Before they headed out, I gave strict instructions that they were to find the three vehicles and, if possible, check them for Graystoke tires, but under no circumstances were they to contact the owners.

Me? My plan was to begin making calls to local tire dealers. I wanted know if any of them had replaced a worn set of Graystoke tires. If they had, I was in trouble. The chances that the dealer still had the old tires were zero.

It was midafternoon when Janet called in with the news that she'd found the 2002 Ford Bronco II belonging to MaryJo Hooks and that it did indeed have Graystoke tires fitted, but only two. The rear wheels sported a shiny new pair of Toyo Proxes size 225/45R17s.

The girl had spotted the Bronco parked outside the woman's home, a ranch style house on Clayton Road in East Brainerd. The hood was up and the engine was being worked on by a man whose face she never did get a glimpse of. What she did see was that he was wearing a black ball cap; she even managed to get a pic of it, but not the logo. Well, she did, but the long lens was shaking so much it was unrecognizable: a round or oval patch, trimmed in white with two, maybe three white letters within the circle, or whatever it was. Apparently, Janet Toliver was something of an amateur photographer and owned a Nikon with a 300mm zoom lens, which is how she was able to figure out the brands of the tires. She'd parked just down the street and photographed one side of the Bronco, and then driven past the house and snapped the other side. And then she handed me the break I'd been looking for: While she was taking the second set of photos, MaryJo had appeared at the front door... with a dog, a chocolate colored wiener. *Holy smoke!*

Janet had managed to snap photos of MaryJo and the dog. *Smart girl. Maybe the chief was right about her after all. Toyo tires, huh? New? Maybe not new enough, but then again... Hell, I deserve a break and right now would be a good time; please,please,please.*

I told her to come on back to the station and get the pics to Mike Willis for printing, and maybe enhancing. Me? I was halfway through calling the tire dealer listings in the Yellow pages. Now, with this new information, I was able to concentrate on just the dealers who sold Toyo tires, unfortunately there were more than a few of them; some, I'd already called and could ignore. The rest... I sighed and picked up the phone, and soon afterwards I got lucky.

On my third call to a tire dealer in Northgate, The Ambler Tire Company, I was reading the name MaryJo Hooks to him, when the guy at the other end of the call, Jubal Johnson, interrupted and told me he remembered her. She'd traded in two Graystoke Tires, rear tires just ten days ago.

Did he still have the old tires? He didn't know, but if I would hold on, he would go check. *Would I hold on? You bet I would.*

He was gone so long I thought he'd forgotten me and I was getting more and more antsy by the minute, until finally:

"Hey, you still there?" he asked.

"Yes, do you have them?"

"Do you have any idea of the size of the pile I had to go through?"

"No. Did you find them?"

"It stretches almost from one end of the building to the other. They was stacked one atop the other..."

"Did? You. Find. *Them?*" I growled.

"Hey, no need to get pissy. Yeah, I found them. They was..."

"I'm sending someone to get them right now. Make sure they're ready when they get there, okay?"

"Well, I dunno. I don't have no authority to..."

"You're the manager, aren't you? Yeah, of course you are. So, if you don't have them ready when my officer arrives to pick them up, I'll have him pick *you* up as well. You have ten minutes. Yes?"

"Yes ma'am."

The tires, when they arrived, were badly worn and of little use. All Mike Willis could say after printing them was that they were similar to the tracks at the scene. No part of them matched the well-defined impressions. The not-so-well-defined impressions? Maybe, but he couldn't say for certain, and that wasn't good enough.

I sat for a moment staring at the dead handset after Mike hung up, then I replaced it, and was soon lost in thought.

Okay, so they are similar, but not an exact match, too worn, almost no tread left, not enough to pass the DOT inspection... Hmmm, so she traded them in. Makes sense! She's not in the habit of having her tires rotated, obviously. So, the front tires... I need to get my hands on them, but how? Maybe...

I leaned forward, picked up the handset, and called the chief.

"Chief Johnston. What do you want, Lieutenant?" *Damn! I do hate caller ID!*

"I need some money, Chief. About a thousand dollars," I said as I closed my eyes and grimaced.

"*You what?*" he yelled. "What the hell for?"

I smiled to myself as I told him.

"I need a new set of tires." Oh, and then he really went off on me. I waited patiently until he'd finished his tirade and then I explained.

"No, not for me…"

"Oh," he said, much more quietly, when I finished telling him my plan. "Oh! Yes, well, we can do that, I think. Do what you have to, Lieutenant, but find that killer—and soon. I'm catching hell from the mayor, the press, and the TBI. They want to take it away from us. I *do not* want that to happen. You understand?"

I did, and I didn't want it either. I had a feeling I was getting close, real close.

I called Ambler Tire back and asked for the manager.

"Jubal Johnson. How can I help you?" It was the same guy I'd talked to before.

"Hello, Jubal. This is Lieutenant Gazzara, remember?" I asked, knowing full well that he would.

"I do. How did those tires work out for you?"

"That's what I want to talk to you about. I need the rest of the set, the two front tires, but I need your help."

"I'm listening."

And so I explained what I had in mind.

He was to call his client and tell her that the two tires he'd sold her ten days earlier were defective. He was to apologize and then tell her that if she would bring the vehicle in, he would replace them; give her four new tires, the extra two as compensation for her inconvenience.

He was silent for a moment, then said, "But there's nothing wrong with the tires we sold her. Toyo are great tires. I don't know if company policy... And then how am I supposed to account for the cost of the four new tires?"

"We'll pay for those," I said. "Call her and make sure you persuade her. Tell her you don't want her riding around on defective tires. Make the appointment, and I'll be there when she arrives, with a check. Just tell me the cost."

It took a little more persuasion, but eventually, he agreed.

Now, what to do about that dog.

The answer to that one came to me while I was in the shower getting ready for bed. That and another call from the pervert.

"Hello, Catherine..."

"Oh, for God's sake. You're just too pathetic."

"What are you wearing, Catherine? Ooh, oooh, ahhhhh, oh, oh jeez... wow!"

"Oh, m'God, are you done already? You need some serious help." I hung up and turned off my phone.

Chapter 21

By the time I arrived at work the following morning, I'd convinced myself that Ball Cap, the man Janet had observed at MaryJo Hooks's house, was both my killer and my nocturnal caller. It was, in part, a gut feeling, but more than that it was because there were just too many coincidences, and I hate those. One is okay, right? Two is stretching the realm of possibility. Three is way over the top, and I had at least five:

1. T.J. Bron had observed a dark colored SUV. MaryJo owns a dark blue Ford Bronco II.

2. The Bronco had Graystoke Weather King tires; we had casts of just such a set of tire impressions found at two of the crime scenes. Whether or not they matched we still had to wait and see. If they did, all doubt was gone. It was him.

3. We had a chocolate wiener dog. Hair from a chocolate wiener had been found on three of the victims. MaryJo has a chocolate wiener dog.

4. Saffron Brooks's last known contact wore a black ball cap. Our man also wore a black ball cap.

5. Two of the victims, that we knew of, had frequented Smart's Gym.

Five coincidences? I think not. It was him. I was sure of it, but I needed more, a lot more, so I waited. I certainly couldn't obtain a search warrant based on that flimsy set of pseudo facts, not even from Harry's tame Federal Judge, Henry Strange. *And he's always had a sweet spot for me too. Bless him.*

The call from Ambler Tire came just a few minutes after ten. Jubal had just gotten off the phone after having set up an appointment with MaryJo Hooks for eleven-thirty that same morning. I told him I'd be there and after putting the phone back on the hook I leaned back in my chair, clasped my hands together behind my neck, stared up at the ceiling, and smiled. *I love it when a plan comes together… Who was it said that? Someone on TV, I think. Eh, who cares? One thing's for sure, though: MaryJo is not my killer, but the guy in the ball cap? He has potential. So, who the hell is this guy with his head stuck under the hood of MaryJo's Bronco?*

I'd had someone watching the house ever since Janet had left. Ball cap had finished whatever it was he was doing to the Bronco and then he'd driven it into the garage and closed the overhead door. He didn't appear again, not that night or the next morning.

I need to get somebody into that house to talk to M.J. without spooking her, or him, but how? I know, the dog. Saturday afternoon? No, today; has to be today. Time is precious. This bastard might strike again, maybe even tonight. I can't let that happen. If it's him, I need to stop him, now!

I leaned forward, picked up my phone, and buzzed Janet.

"I need you to go home," I said, then noted the look on her face as I watched her through the office window, and laughed, "No, no. It's nothing like that. I need you to go and change into something casual: jeans and a t-shirt; something like that..." I thought for a moment, *she can't do this alone. She needs a buddy.*

"Hold that thought," I said as I put her on hold and punched in another number.

"Peck, Traffic."

"Captain Peck," I said. "It's me again. I need a female officer, a young one. Can you help?"

He could and he did. I had Janet come to my office; rookie Officer Leslie Jenkins arrived just a few minutes later.

I filled them both in on my plan and then sent them home to change and do some shopping. I'd told them to come back to my office for a final briefing. I figured they'd be back by noon.

MaryJo Hooks—she'd taken the bait—though she didn't know it, was now a VIP customer at Ambler; Jubal was keeping a bay open especially for her. She arrived early for her appointment. She was alone, unaccompanied, even by the dog.

The tires were duly changed, and when she left, she was obviously happy with her windfall. The two front tires were taken into custody and I delivered them to Mike Willis, who promised me an answer no later than mid-day on Monday. I wasn't too happy about that, but I had to put up with it. These weren't fingerprints we were dealing with; they were a whole lot bigger and much less well-defined, and whatever Mike found, or didn't find, we had to be certain of the result. If his inspection came back positive, it had to stand up in court.

So, with the tires now in safe hands, all four of them, I returned to my office and my two fledgling pet groomers. Yes, good or bad, that was my plan.

I wired Janet with an earpiece and microphone—the earpiece tucked away under her hair, the mike hidden inside her bra. I wouldn't be able to see anything, but I would be able to hear what was going on inside the house, should they be able to gain access, and to give her instructions.

Would the plan work? Would it get us a look inside the house, and maybe even a glimpse of the elusive Ball Cap? Who knew? Not me, that was for sure. What I had going for me were two young women with bubbly personalities and a winning way with words... well, Janet did. Leslie? I didn't know her that well. Okay, it was iffy. Would MaryJo go for it? I didn't know. I knew I wouldn't, not these days, but then I'm a cop and I know the dangers of letting strangers into my house.

Then I had another thought: if this guy in the ball cap was indeed my killer, I could be putting these two young women in danger, and that bothered me, a lot. So, I spent a few extra minutes warning them. I finished by telling them both that they could say no, that they didn't want to do it, and I would understand, that there would be no recriminations.

They both smiled at me and said they were ready, so I repeated my instructions, then they climbed aboard their van—borrowed from Doc Sheddon—and away we went.

***

We, that is, they, arrived outside the house on Clayton Road at ten after two. Frost parked the unmarked cruiser half a block away on an adjoining street, behind a similar unmarked running stakeout, and from where we had a view of the parked van. The Bronco was nowhere to be seen.

"Must be inside the garage," Frost said, peering through his binoculars. "Either that, or he's out somewhere."

"Hold that thought," I said, exiting the vehicle.

I went to the stakeout car and had a few words with the two detectives therein, and then returned to my own car.

"No. He's in there. Those two say they took over from the night shift at seven this morning and, other than MaryJo's comings and goings, they've seen nothing. He hasn't made an appearance since Janet saw him yesterday."

"You don't suppose he made her, do you?" Frost asked. "She's a real rookie. Nice kid and willing to do what it takes, but she has no experience."

"That's too true," I said as I turned on the coms, "He could have, I suppose," I now had my field glasses to my eyes, "but I'd hate to think so, especially with her going into that house... Okay, here we go. Janet. Can you hear me?"

"Loud and clear, Boss."

"Good, are you ready?"

"We are."

"Okay, let's do it."

It was difficult to see what was happening, but I heard her knocking on the door.

The door must have opened, because I heard Janet say, "Oh how lovely. A chocolate dachshund. I love those... Oh dear. I'm sorry. My name is Janet and this is Leslie. We're starting a new mobile pet grooming business. Do you take him to a groomer?"

"No, I don't," MaryJo said. "And this is Sadie May, she's a girl."

"Oh, I'm so sorry. I couldn't see because of the way you're holding her." She giggled, then continued, "Hello, Sadie May. What a beautiful name. So, you don't use a groomer. Well, this is your lucky day, Ms. ..."

"Hooks, MaryJo Hooks. Why is it my lucky day?"

"Because we're trying to start a new business and we're giving away free services to potential new clients. We'll bathe Sadie May for you, clip her toenails, and give her a nice brushing, all for free. She'll love it."

"Oh, m'God," I said, "clip her nails. Don't overdo it, Janet."

"Oh, I don't know about that," MaryJo said. "I really can't afford to pay a groomer, and you'll want to see her every week."

"No, not at all. Once a month is what we recommend, and we only charge $20, less if we get enough customers in the area. So how about it? The first one is free. Oh pleeease? Sadie May would love it. You know she would."

"Now shut up," I said, frantically. "Wait her out. The first one that speaks loses."

And she did just that, she didn't say another word until MaryJo finally gave in.

"Oh... I suppose... Okay then, if it's free, and I'm not making any promises about future visits."

"That's fine. Can we come in then? Oh goody. Thank you soooo much. Leslie, why don't you go get the bag from the van and we'll get started."

I watched as Janet stepped inside the house and Leslie went back to the van; then she too disappeared into the house.

192

We listened as the two girls chatted together and went about bathing the dog.

"Make sure you get some dog hairs when you dry her," I whispered.

"Well hell-oh," a man's voice said. "And what are two lovely girls such as yourselves doing wasting your time grooming dogs?"

"It's him, Janet," I whispered. "Play him along, flirt with him." *Oh my God. What am I telling them to do?*

"No, don't flirt with him, just see if you can get him to talk, but for God's sake be careful. If he's our boy, he's a wicked SOB."

"Larry, what are you doing?" The question came from MaryJo.

'Larry?' I mouthed to Frost. He shrugged.

"Janet," I whispered, "play him a little. See if you can get his last name."

"Larry?" Janet said. "I had an uncle called Larry. At least that's what my mother said he was, my uncle. Turned out he was her favorite squeeze." She laughed, giggled. MaryJo laughed too, and so did Larry.

"Would you believe he tried to seduce me?" Janet asked. "One night, he came and got into bed with me. I dunno what would have happened if

193

mom hadn't burst in on us. She kicked uncle Larry out after that. He really was quite nice... though, and I've often wondered... well, you know," she said, wistfully.

"What the hell are you doing?" I whispered. Obviously, I didn't get an answer. "Stop it."

"There now, Sadie May," Janet said. "All done. All nice and dry. I hope you like the service, Mrs. Hooks, and you too, Mr. Hooks."

"It's Jackson, Larry Jackson. MaryJo and I are not married. Not yet, we're engaged." *Oh m'God. Well done, you little minx.*

"And yes, we'd like to see you both again," he said. "Can we have your number please?"

She gave it to him, said it out loud as she wrote it down for him; at least I assumed she wrote it down.

Ten minutes later they were out in the van, loaded and pulling away. I went to the surveillance car and told them to stay put, and that if Larry Jackson left the house they were to let me know and follow him.

Me? I was ecstatic. We had dog hairs—at least I hoped we did—for comparison, and we had Ball Cap's name. We also had tire imprints. If they matched, I'd get a search warrant.

"Janet, are you still hearing me?" I asked as Frost eased the unmarked away from the curb. "What the hell were you trying to do in there? What was all that crap about your uncle?"

I heard her giggle as she said, "You should have seen his face. It was a picture. You said to play him. That's what I was doing. Did I go too far?"

"Yes, dammit! You certainly did go too far. If he's our killer, you may have just provided him with his next target. 'You often wondered,' oh, m'God, Janet."

"I had you all going, didn't I? But we did get the goods. I have plenty of doggy hairs—Sadie May is the sweetest little soul. I could have squeezed her to death—and I got his name. How cool is that?"

I had to admit it: it was pretty cool, no, it was more than that. The way she drew it out of him was pretty damn smart.

I told her to deliver the dog hairs to Mike Willis and then to go home and get some rest; I'd see them both bright and early in the morning. And then I took my own advice and had Frost drop me off at my car in the lot on Amnicola and I headed home too.

I was in a good... no, I was in a great mood when I arrived home that evening. It was the best I'd felt since the night I got the call to Saffron's crime scene, now more than two months ago.

I turned up the heat, poured myself two fingers of a very special and expensive scotch whisky—a birthday gift from Harry Starke some four years ago—and flopped down on the sofa and celebrated my exceptional day. Later I made myself a chicken salad sandwich, opened a bottle of red, and then I took a nice, long hot shower. By nine o'clock I was in bed with my iPad to read a little and have a good long sleep.

I hadn't been in bed fifteen minutes when my iPhone buzzed on the nightstand. I groaned, *Oh, no. Not again. Give me a break.*

Well, I wasn't going to let the pervert spoil my day. I flipped the screen and held the phone to my ear.

"I was waiting for you," I whispered. "Talk to me."

"Whadda ya mean, you was waiting for me?"

"Oh m'God," I laughed as I sat upright. "I'm sorry, Lonnie. I thought you were someone else."

"Damn," he said. "You sounded hot. Who's the lucky guy?"

"No one you'd know. How's it going now that you're a civilian? Are you feeling any better?"

"I'm good. Look, I was just thinking about you; thought I'd give you a call. How are you, Kate?"

"I'm fine, but you sound down. Is everything okay?"

In my mind, knowing him as well as I did, I saw him shrug, "I hate to admit it, but I miss you guys... especially you, Kate."

"Awe, that's sweet of you. Tell you what. I'm almost done with the case I'm working—you remember, the Saffron Brooks case. Anyway, let me get it cleared and I'll let you buy me lunch. Good?"

I could see his smile.

"Yeah, that's good. I'll hold you to it. You want to tell me about the case?"

I didn't, but we talked for several minutes more... no, we talked for another hour, and then I told him goodnight, turned out the light, and slept like the dead until my alarm woke me at six o'clock.

The perv didn't call that night. I must admit that I was a little disappointed, not.

Chapter 22

It was just after eight the following morning when I walked into my office. Guess who was waiting for me. Yep, Assistant Chief Finkle. He was seated behind my desk, his elbows on the arms of the chair, his fingers laced together in front of him. *Wow, thank God I locked my desk drawers.*

"Good morning, Chief," I said, as I hung my jacket on its hook behind the door, and then sat down on one of my own guest chairs in front of the desk. "You're early. What can I do for you?"

"I understand that you've found your killer. When are you going to make the arrest? I'll need to call a press conference."

"Er, don't you think that's a little premature? I'm not even sure it's him yet... Who have you been talking to?"

"I talked to Detective Frost on my way in to see you. He was most helpful." *When you twisted his arm, I bet.* "So, I'll ask you again: when are you going to arrest Jackson?"

"I'm still waiting for the results of several tests; namely the tire imprints, the DNA that LT. Willis pulled from the cigarette paper, and now the dog hairs. If I get a positive result on any one of them, I'll get a warrant and search the house. That good enough for you?"

"No, Lieutenant, it's not. You need to arrest him, immediately. If another girl dies, and you could have stopped it, your career will be over, and I will make damned sure that it is. You got me?"

"Yes, I do got you, but I can't arrest him... not yet. What I have is all circumstantial. Yes, I think it's him. It certainly *could* be him, but 'could' is not good enough. I have no physical evidence to link him to any one of the five victims—not yet anyway. I need some solid evidence. A match between the tires and cast of the imprints would do it, but I'm still waiting for Lieutenant Willis to confirm that, or not. I'm having Jackson watched around the clock, but there's nothing more I can do until something gives."

"Well, it'd better be soon. As I said, if there's another death, the media will crucify us, and don't think I won't throw you to the wolves; I will. *Get it done, Lieutenant.*" And then he got up out of my seat and was gone.

Me? I got up too, went to the door and beckoned for Frost, Janet, and Leslie—yes, Captain Peck had turned her loose for the duration—to join me, and I went and sat down behind my desk. The chair was still warm, and I shuddered in disgust at the thought of his skinny ass. So I rose again and turned to my big board, grabbed the black marker and wrote at the top center, 'Lawrence? Larry Jackson.' By the time I'd done that my team was all present.

"Okay, people," I said after they'd seated themselves, "the first thing we need to do is run a background check on Larry Jackson..."

"Already done," Frost interrupted me.

I was impressed, "Oh yeah? Okay, so tell us."

He opened his iPad, flipped through the screens, and began.

"He does have a criminal record, it's not much, but it's significant and relevant to this case. First, there's an arrest warrant for him out in California; a parole violation.

"Second, in 2007 he was sentenced to ten years in a San Diego prison for twice raping his former wife. He was paroled and released from prison in 2013 after serving six years. He skipped out of California six months later.

"And third, he's now listed there as a sexual sadist, a person who likes to inflict pain on his sexual partner in order to gain sexual satisfaction for himself.

"That's it. There's nothing more. Nothing since he did a runner from California. He has a Tennessee driver's license issued in Polk County in 2015. The address listed is 6217 Clayton Road. So it would appear he's been living with Ms. Hooks at least since then."

I listened to him without interrupting. The rapes of his first wife and subsequent prison stretch were a shocking development and, as Frost had said, they were significant, but that's all. Coincidence? Not hardly. Evidence? No. Just because he was into rape and inflicting pain didn't mean he was a killer. Significant? Of course. Added to what we already had, it made me more certain than ever that Larry Jackson was our man, but I still couldn't *prove* it. I needed more. I needed hard evidence linking him to the crime scenes.

I didn't get it until two days later, on Saturday morning.

Chapter 23

For two more days I kept the surveillance team in place and working the house on Clayton Road. MaryJo Hooks left a couple of times, but I had the team stay put. It was Jackson I wanted them to keep an eye on. My theory being, even if they were working together, God forbid, she wouldn't do anything untoward by herself. I was wrong.

On Saturday morning, two things happened. The first frightened the crap out of me. At nine o'clock that morning, Janet came rushing into my office to tell me she'd had a phone call from MaryJo: she wanted Janet to come back to the house that afternoon to bathe the dog.

"But it's only been four days," I said. "What the hell's going on?"

"I don't know," her face was white.

"Janet, you look awful. What's wrong?"

"She, she wants me to come alone."

That took my breath away. *Oh my God. They* are *working together. Holy shit! They're after Janet.*

"Don't worry," I said. "That's not going to happen."

202

"I told her I'd do it," Janet said, "but that I'd call her back to confirm."

And then the second thing happened: I spotted Mike Willis hurrying through the incident room.

"Just a minute, Janet. Oh, and no way are you to do anything or confirm anything without talking to me first. Let's see what Mike wants and then we'll deal with it."

The door burst open and he rushed in.

"Got 'em!" he shouted, loud enough to turn heads all the way across the floor to the elevator doors. "It's a match. The left front tire. It matches the cast." He slapped the imprinted white paper down in front of me. The black tireprint was covered with small yellow circles. I looked up at him as he reared over my desk, my eyebrows raised in question. I may have looked calm, but inside I was absolutely boiling with excitement.

"See these," he pointed to the yellow circles, "the accidental characteristics, they match... Kate, you've got what you need."

I looked at the print, then up at him, "You sure, Mike? I don't need to screw this up. Finkle would have a conniption, and my job."

He nodded, "Yes, I'm sure. So, what we have here are nine matching points, including the damned rock, this one," he pointed to a double yellow circle surrounding something I couldn't identify. "It's still stuck in the damned tire." Oh, he was excited.

"You've got him, Kate!" he shouted, throwing his arms up in the air. "You've got your killer. This is direct physical evidence, and I'll swear to it in court."

It was what he said before that that brought me down: 'You've got your killer.' I had the evidence, true enough, but not the killer, not now that I knew MaryJo was involved. We still had no proof that Larry Jackson was the killer. All we knew was that the tires on MaryJo's Ford Bronco II matched the imprints found at the scene where Melody Ferber's body was discovered. It could be just him, and deep down I was sure it was, but MaryJo's phone call to Janet had thrown a whole different light on it. She, MaryJo, working alone, could have been the killer, but it also could have been both of them acting together. We still had a lot of work to do. But I wasn't about to kill Mike's euphoria. He deserved a big pat on the back.

"Okay," I said, standing up and offering him my hand. "I love you, buddy, and thank you. I'll get a warrant to search the house."

I looked over his shoulder to where Janet was still standing, "Maybe you can keep your appointment after all," and I smiled at her. She smiled back, tentatively.

"Oh, don't worry," I said, as I looked at my watch. It was almost ten o'clock. "You won't be by yourself. Now, I need to be alone, at least for a few minutes while I make a phone call."

I waited until the door closed before I picked up my iPhone and punched in a number, and then I waited. By the fourth ring I was beginning to feel really antsy. This was my only option to secure a warrant almost immediately, one that couldn't be argued with, by anybody. Finally, he picked up.

"Henry Strange."

"Judge... Henry, it's Kate Gazzara. I need a big, no, a really big favor."

"And hello, how are you too, Kate," he said, the sarcasm heavy in his voice.

"Oh, Henry, I'm sorry. I didn't mean... oh, m'God, Henry, I need a warrant and I need it now. I have a serial killer on my hands and he's... she's... or both are after one of my officers. Would you do it for me, please?"

"You have probable cause, I presume."

"That I do, Henry," and without doing so at length, I outlined what I had.

"Well then, my dear, come on over."

"Thank you, Henry. You've no idea how much I appreciate it."

He laughed and disconnected.

***

I began again to gather my stuff together and was just about to leave to go get the warrant when my iPhone rang.

It was Assistant Chief Finkle.

"What are you doing, Lieutenant? I need a progress report," he said. *No hello? Damn!*

"I'm almost there, Chief. I have a match on the tires, and I'm on my way to pick up a search warrant for the house in East Brainerd. I gotta go. Talk to you later."

"Yes, much later, *Catherine,*" he whispered. And then, with a low laugh, he hung up.

What? And then it hit me, and I was so stunned, I was speechless, *Son... Of... A... Bitch... It was you! You freakin' pervert.*

I was so surprised, and horrified, I almost fell back into my seat. As it was, I dropped down with a thump.

Oh, my, God. Finkle. It was freakin' Finkle. What the hell am I going to do?

But I couldn't think about it, not then. My mind had gone blank, utterly and completely blank.

Oh shit! I've gotta figure it out. I can't...

But the thoughts wouldn't come, and I had other things to do.

I grabbed the rest of my stuff and hurried out the door. As I rushed through the incident room, I stopped and told Frost to get ready to search the house, and then I told Janet to make the call to MaryJo and confirm an appointment for two o'clock that afternoon. That done, I headed to my car to go get my warrant.

Once I was in my cruiser and on the road, my head began to clear and I was able to think. I was almost to Judge Strange's offices when I had the idea:

Oh wow, yeah. That would do it... Nah, you can't do that; it's way over the top, and he wouldn't go for it anyway. Yes, he would. His ego... It sounded good in theory, but right then it was just a fantasy, and I really wasn't sure it would work. It would take a lot more figuring out before it became a plan.

Chapter 24

We arrived at the house on Clayton Road in force. My team included Janet, Jack Frost, Leslie, and a half-dozen uniforms. We traveled in three cars and the van. Janet parked the van in front of the house. I, along with Frost and Leslie, waited out of sight in the back of the van. The three unmarked cruisers parked on an adjoining street. Janet was wired as before.

Why didn't we just bust in through the door? I must admit, I wasn't sure if I was doing the right thing, but I still didn't know what MaryJo was up to. I wanted more information. My idea was for Janet to go in while we waited outside and recorded the conversation. If they made a move on her, we'd know, and we'd move fast. But, as he always does, Mr. Murphy decided to take a hand in the proceedings—you do know Murphy's Law, right? Well, just in case you don't, it states, 'Whatever can go wrong, will go wrong'—and things went south fast, right from the minute she walked in the door.

"Hello, my dear," MaryJo said when she opened the door. "It's so nice to see you. Do come in."

The door closed; we listened.

"Does anyone know you're here?" MaryJo asked.

"Um, no, not really."

"Oh hell," I said, more to myself than the others inside the van. "Wrong answer."

"Not really?" MaryJo asked. "What does that mean?"

"Er, um, no. Nobody."

"Ah, I see. Shall we go in here. Sadie May's waiting for you."

I looked at Frost, slowly shaking my head, hoping to hell that what I most feared wasn't really happening.

"We need to get in there, now," he said.

I nodded. This was no time to wait. It only takes seconds to render someone unconscious, and only minutes to strangle them.

"Let's do it," I said, but Frost was already out of the van and running for the door. He didn't stop. He hit that door like a defensive tackle taking down Brett Favre. The door didn't stand a chance. The lock smashed through the frame, the door flew open, and Frost staggered headlong into the house. I was only a second behind him. I ran in, my Glock in both hands at the ready, followed by Leslie in close support, her gun also in hand.

We were in the hallway; the house was silent. Of the three doors that led off the hallway, two were open, the third closed. There was no sign of Janet, MaryJo, or Jackson. I nodded at the closed door, Frost nodded back, reached out a hand and tried the knob. The door was locked. *Damn!* Frost reared back and with a single kick the door burst open, and he continued on through into the room. Again, I, followed by Leslie, ran in after him, to be greeted by a sight I never want to see again.

Janet was on her knees, head down resting on the floor, steadying herself with one hand and holding her throat with the other, a piece of knotted rope lay beside her.

MaryJo was seated, weeping loudly, on the sofa under a window that opened onto the driveway between the house and the garage. It was open and there was no sign of Larry Jackson. *Shit!*

I rushed to Janet's side while Frost jerked the distraught woman to her feet and cuffed her.

Janet turned her head sideways and looked up at me, and to my relief, she smiled.

"We got 'em, Boss," she whispered, her voice raspy. "We got 'em," then she passed out and fell sideways onto the floor. *Oh shit, no!*

I felt her pulse and heaved a sigh of relief. It was strong; she'd only fainted. And then I heard the roar of an engine. I didn't have to look to see who or what it was, I could guess. Larry Jackson was making a getaway, but I wasn't concerned; I knew he wouldn't get far. Jack Frost was already making the call.

Janet came round a few moments later and sat up, holding her throat. Gently, I pulled her hand away; there were two huge bruises, three inches apart, on the front of her neck and red, raw contusions that ran from the front to the back on each side. She also had a large bruise on her left cheek. We had arrived not a second too soon.

I turned to Frost, "Call an ambulance. She needs to go to the hospital."

"No I don't," she rasped. "I'm fine. Just give me a minute, okay?"

I rolled my eyes at Frost, "Make the call, Jack." And he did.

"Janet, you sit over here and wait for the paramedics," I said, helping her up.

I turned to the still weeping MaryJo Hooks. She looked pathetic. I sat down on the sofa beside her, set my iPhone to record, then placed it on the coffee table in front of her.

"MaryJo," I said quietly, "from now on, our conversation will be recorded. I am going to take the cuffs off and then I'm going to read you your rights." I took them off and continued, "Please listen carefully and don't say anything until I'm finished."

I took a deep breath and then began, "MaryJo Hooks, I am arresting you for the murders of..."

"*I didn't!*" she screamed. "I didn't kill anybody. It was him. It was Larry!" and she began to sob uncontrollably.

Gently, I put my hand on her arm, "Please. MaryJo, listen to me. I'm arresting you for the murders of Saffron Brooks, Cindy Clarke, and Melody Ferber. You have the right to remain silent..." and so on, until finally, "Do you understand these rights?"

She nodded, tears still streaming down her face.

"I need you to say yes or no, out loud, for the record, please."

"Yes, I understand them, but I didn't do anything. I didn't kill anyone. It was him. He did it," she wept.

I nodded, "With these rights in mind, are you willing to talk to me?" It's sad but true that at this point most people waive their rights, and MaryJo did just that.

"Yes. He hurt me. Look."

She stood and pulled up her t-shirt, exposing her chest. From breasts to waist, she was covered in what looked like cigarette burns. There must have been a hundred of them. It was sickening.

"I never did anything," she continued. "I never touched those girls. He said he'd kill *me* if I didn't help him. He brought them here. I just talked to them, is all. I swear," and she burst into tears again.

It was at that point that Sadie May made an appearance. MaryJo gathered her up into her arms, cuddled her, then turned her loose. The dog waded through the cushions to the arm of the sofa, climbed up on it, and then stuck its nose into the ashtray on the side table. Sadie May snuffled around among the butts, selected a large one, then jumped down to the floor and ran off with it.

"Oh dear," MaryJo said, sniffling and wiping her nose on a tissue. "I should have put that ashtray on the coffee table, where she couldn't get at it," and she did just that, then continued, "Poor Sadie May is addicted to nicotine. She chews them up, makes a terrible mess."

I stared at her in astonishment and asked, "She's addicted to nicotine?"

"Yes. She's been at the ashtrays for years, loves her fix."

I looked at Frost. He was grinning like a fool.

I turned again to MaryJo, "I have a warrant to search the house. I'm going to have my officers do that now. In the meantime, Detective Frost will take you to the police department."

"Oh please, don't take me away. What will happen to Sadie May? I can't leave her. She needs me."

"Don't worry about her. I'll make sure she's okay."

I nodded to Frost. He took her arm and helped her to her feet, and then he gently escorted her out.

We searched the house from top to bottom. We found several sets of car keys in a dresser drawer in Jackson's room. One of them was for a Honda CRV, which I assumed had belonged to Saffron. The keys, along with the rope Jackson had used in his attempt to strangle Janet, were bagged and tagged. Sadie May, so it seemed, liked to enjoy her smoke—chew, that is—under one of the beds. She chewed up the butt and came out from under the bed, then began rooting around for more. I found a pet taxi in the garage and housed her temporarily in that. What I was going to do with her, I had no idea.

The bedroom where she took her fix, however, turned up some interesting evidence: The bed—it wasn't actually a bed, it was a fold out—was positioned on a large, inexpensive off-white area rug with a wide fringe. Under the bed, the floor was literally covered in chewed up ciggy's; beyond the bed, it was littered with tiny fragments of white filter paper. *So, this is where he did it,* I thought, as I watched the crime scene tech carefully vacuum every inch of the rug. *He strangled them until they were unconscious, then stripped them naked. What he did with them then, god only knows, but sooner or later they ended up on the rug, naked and dead, and that's where they picked up the fibers, dog hairs, and fragments of paper.*

I shook my head as I stared down at the rug. Whatever did those poor girls go through? Nightmares would be nothing compared to what this monster must have put them through.

I didn't stay until the search was completed—it took the rest of that day, and all of the next. I stayed for an hour and then I had a cruiser take me back to the PD. I was tired, depressed. I needed a drink and I wanted to go home. Unfortunately, I couldn't. I still had to finish

215

interviewing MaryJo, and Larry Jackson was still on the run.

MaryJo was in an interview room, sitting at the table nursing a cup of coffee. She'd lawyered up by the time I got there; a young public defender, whom I knew vaguely, was seated beside her with a large yellow legal pad and an iPad set on the table in front of her. I sighed and pushed open the door.

"Hello, MaryJo," I said, as I sat down on the opposite side of the table. "Lucy," I said, and nodded to the public defender, who nodded back.

And so, the dance began. I turned on the camera and recorder, re-read MaryJo her rights, and battling constant interruptions from Lucy, I dragged her story out of her. Unfortunately, the two hours I spent doing it added very little to what she'd already told me. In short, she did little more than talk to the girls—under duress, of course—and it was Jackson, alone, who raped and killed them.

Lucy—for the life of me I can't remember her last name—insisted on having MaryJo strip down to her underwear for the camera in order to make a record of her injuries and to show that she only did what she did because she was forced to. It was a horrible sight, and one I knew would generate a lot of sympathy with a jury. The front of her body, from neck to bikini line, was covered in burns. To the rear, it was the same, only worse. Her back was covered in, not only burns, but also long, red welts, which she said were made by Jackson when he whipped her, and that he did it often.

It was at that point I gave up on the interview. That she did what she did while under duress was evident, but still I wondered... Whatever. I had enough evidence to arrest her for first degree murder, even knowing that the DA would probably change it to something lesser.

They captured Larry Jackson that same evening in Hamilton County.

Chapter 25

I was in bed and asleep when the call came in. I picked up my phone from the nightstand. It was two-fifteen and I didn't recognize the number. I almost ignored the call, and not for one minute did I think Finkle was up to his tricks again, but I had a feeling I needed to take it. It was Detective Ron Akers. They had Jackson locked up in the county jail. Apparently, a deputy running radar on Highway 58 had spotted the dark blue Bronco heading north toward Harrison. He called for backup and then engaged in a high-speed pursuit that ended when Jackson made a hard right onto Harrison Ooltewah Road, misjudged the turn, left the road, clipped a tree, and finally rolled the unstable vehicle onto its roof. Fortunately, Jackson wasn't hurt, but the Bronco was totaled.

I arrived at the Hamilton County Sheriff's Department at a little after eight that morning; Detectives Akers and Flowers were waiting for me.

"Detectives," I said when they met me in reception. "You have my boy, then? Good job."

"We have *our* boy," Flowers growled. "We want him for the Perez killing." *Why am I not surprised?*

I rewarded him with my sweetest smile, "I'm sure you do, Gene, but without evidence or

218

probable cause you can only hold him for twenty-four hours. Since you don't have hard evidence, and I don't have it, not for the Perez case, then we have nothing to tie him to it, other than a strong suspicion. I, on the other hand, *can* tie him to three murders, all within the city limits, so I'm here to arrest him. Now, can I go get him?"

Flowers grunted something I didn't quite hear.

"Excuse me?" I asked.

"Nothing, nothing," he said, "but I sure do hope you have enough to charge him. He's a mean SOB."

"Oh, I do, believe me. I do. Now, one more time: can we go get him?"

"Sure we can," Akers said, grinning at me. "This way, if you please." *Now that's more like it.*

They led me back through a labyrinth of corridors to an interview room where the suspect was being held.

The first thing I thought when I looked through the glass into the interview room was, *Oh my God, he's gorgeous.* And he was.

I found out later that he was just over six feet tall, but even though he was seated he looked taller. He sat with his back rigid, his hands cuffed to the table, his head held high, his gaze straight forward, his eyes half-closed, and lips set in a tight straight line. It was truly a handsome face, a movie star's face, topped with brown hair that had obviously been cut and styled by a professional. *Wow, Ted Bundy rides again.*

"He's not talking," Flowers said, "other than to demand an attorney. You wanna try?"

"That I do, but I don't care if he does or doesn't. I'm arresting him. Will you join me?" I asked, more to keep the peace than a need for help.

They did, and together we entered the room.

"Mr. Jackson," Akers said. "Allow me to introduce you to a lady I imagine you'll be seeing quite a lot of from now on. This is Lieutenant Catherine Gazzara, Chattanooga Police Department."

"I know who she is," he snapped. "Where's my freakin' attorney?"

"Lawrence Jackson," I began, "I'm arresting you for the murders of Saffron Brooks, Cindy Clarke, and Melody Ferber. You have the right to remain silent…"

"Screw you, Bitch," he interrupted me. "I want an attorney."

220

Gene Flowers took a step forward, his fist raised, "That's no freaking way to talk to a lady, you sick son of a..." I put my hand out to restrain him.

"It's okay, Gene. I can handle him."

"Like hell, you can," he growled.

I ignored him and continued to read Jackson his rights. He ignored me, remained staring stoically at the far wall of the interview room.

Outside, on the other side of the one-way glass, I turned to the two county detectives and said, "I'll need a full set of restraints—wrists, waist, ankles, the works. I'll make sure you get them back..."

"And see that you do," a booming voice said from the doorway. "If not," Sheriff White said with a huge grin, "I'll come after you myself."

I smiled at him, "And you'd always be welcome, Whitey."

He laughed, then turned serious, "So that's him, right?"

I nodded and said, "That's what the evidence tells us. I just charged him with..."

"I know, I heard you," he interrupted me. "Good job, Lieutenant. Call me if you need to."

And with that, he left us to finish trussing Jackson up.

"You want me to ride with you?" Flowers asked. "I told you; he's mean."

"Oh for God's sake. No! It's only a couple of miles. I think I can handle it. Look at him, he's not going anywhere I don't take him. Let's get him out of here." And we did.

"Thank you, boys," I said to the two detectives, through the car window as I pulled away. "See you soon. Give me a call, anytime."

"Anytime?" Akers asked, with a sly smile.

"Give it up, Ron," I said, smiling back at him. "It ain't never gonna happen."

"I can dream, Kate. I can dream."

Oh, I was in a good mood as I drove to Amnicola, so good in fact, I figured it was time to put my little plan into action. As soon as I got back to my office and had Larry Jackson squared away in a holding cell, I sat down at my desk, then took a deep breath. It was time. I made the call.

**

It was more than thirty minutes later when Assistant Chief Finkle finally made an appearance. As always, he entered my office without bothering to knock. *What is it with that?* I wondered. *Even*

Chief Johnston knocks. Must be one of those screw you things, I suppose.

"So," he said, sitting down in front of my desk. "Talk to me. How's it going?"

"I assume you are asking about the investigation, not my health," I said, dryly. He didn't seem to notice.

"Of course, the investigation. What else would I be asking about?"

"Well, I'm surprised you haven't heard. We have Jackson safely locked away downstairs. I've arrested him for the murders of..." and then I spent the next thirty minutes or so bringing him up to date. He sat quietly, listening, nodding now and again, but saying nothing.

Finally, when I was done, he took a deep breath, put both hands on the arms of his chair, pushed up, and rose to his feet.

"I suppose I should congratulate you," he said. "So, congratulations, Lieutenant. Keep me informed," he said, and turned to leave.

"Er, if you wouldn't mind, Sir," I said, "there's one other... well, if you've got a minute."

He looked down at me across the desk, then frowned and sat down again.

"Make it quick. I don't have all night."

I made sure no one was near my office door or windows, and then said, "Look, Chief," as I picked up my phone, "I think maybe I..." I looked at him wide-eyed, the picture of innocence, I hoped. "I think I screwed up, pissed you off..." I waited. He said nothing, just sat staring at me.

I looked down at the table, took a deep breath, one I hoped he saw, then said, "I meant what I said, about not dating within the department but..."

I paused again, stared at him, as if I wasn't sure what I wanted to say next. I tried to look fearful, which I wasn't. I don't know how well I played it, but he seemed to go for it.

He narrowed his eyes, folded his arms, frowned again, and said, "So? What are you trying to say?"

I shrugged, "Well, I thought... I..." I paused again, looked down at my iPhone, pretended to fidget with it. When I looked up again, I said, somewhat defiantly, "I thought maybe we could go for a drink... perhaps." I looked down again, pretending I was unable to look him in the eye.

I looked up at him. He cocked his head to one side. His eyes narrowed even further, until they were mere slits.

"Give me that," he snatched the phone away from me, looked at it, then flung it down on the desk.

"Just a drink," I added hurriedly. "That's all."

He continued to glare at me.

"Well, what do you say?" I asked, trying to sound worried.

"What brought this on, Lieutenant? What's your game?"

"Nothing. No game, I just thought... well, I just thought that maybe I'd gotten it wrong. You did say you wanted us to get to know each other, and that usually means only one thing. Then I thought about it; you are married, after all and... well, what the hell? What harm can a couple of drinks do? And... well, this situation between us, it's not good. I, that is we, need to get along... don't we?" I paused, lowered my head a little, looked him right in the eye through my eyelashes, and said, softly, "And then there were the phone calls..."

"Phone calls? What phone calls?"

"Well, you know... Damn it, Henry. I know you made them. Do I have to spell it out for you? They turned me on, okay?" I almost shouted that last bit at him.

He sucked his top lip underneath his bottom lip, stared at me some more, his eyes still hidden by the lids, then slowly he nodded.

"All right. Drinks, then. When? Where?"

I looked at my watch, "It's after six now. How about I go home and freshen up and then meet you say... at eight; at the Sorbonne? We'll celebrate the arrest, yes?" And then I waited.

"The Sorbonne? Are you out of your mind? That place is a rat's nest."

I cocked my head and looked at him, coquettishly.

"Oh, it's not so bad. It's quiet up until about ten, and it's unlikely we'll see anyone we know there. We can be... well, you know." *That's enough, Kate,* I thought. *Don't overdo it.*

His eyes widened and the corners of his mouth turned up into a smile. I almost shuddered. I've seen nicer looks on a Pitbull.

"I'm glad you've come around. You won't regret it. The Sorbonne, then; at eight." He stood, walked to the door, opened it, then turned and said, "I look forward to it... Catherine," and then he was gone.

I let out my breath with a whoosh, watched him through my office window until the incident room door closed behind him, and then I called the Sorbonne. Benny answered on the third ring.

"Sorbonne, where every night is party night."

Oh, m'God. How appropriate is that? I almost laughed out loud, but I didn't.

"Benny. It's Kate Gazzara. I need a favor. Well, what I really need is a little help. Can you get Laura on the on the other line?"

He could and he did.

I explained what I needed as Benny wheezed with laughter, and then he said, "I love it, but he won't go for it. He'll know you're up to something."

"He already has," I said. "I'm meeting him in the bar at eight. I will be suitably late, of course."

Laura simply said, "Way. To. Go. Kate. Of course we will."

I arrived home thirty minutes later and laid out my clothes for the evening. I looked down at them laying there on the bed and I smiled to myself. *You're wicked, Kate.*

An hour later, I was dressed and ready to go. I took one last look in the mirror and smiled at myself. My hair was loose and fell four inches below my shoulders. I was wearing a low-cut, little black dress with a flared skirt, and matching shoes with four-inch heels. Those, I was a little worried about. Finkle was only five-eight. Those heels pushed me up to more than six-three. *Ah, screw it. He'll either like the look or he won't and I don't give a damn either way. Yeah, you're lookin' good, girl.*

I was late. *Of course I was.* There's nothing better than keeping a man waiting to put him on the defensive.

I parked on the side street adjoining Prospect, left my coat in the car, and walked around the corner and through the entrance to the Sorbonne.

The joint was just about empty when I walked in: a single couple seated in one of the booths, and Finkle seated at the bar. He was wearing a white shirt, jeans, a black leather jacket, and loafers. He looked quite presentable.

Benny spotted me as soon as I entered. I could tell because of the long, low wolf whistle, "Wow," he sounded impressed. "Now there's a sight for sore eyes. You look beautiful, Kate."

By then, Finkle had turned on his stool and was staring wide-eyed at me—hell, he was almost drooling. I sashayed across the empty room, making sure the skirt of that little black number

228

swished as I walked, and sat down on the stool beside him, my skirt riding up my thighs as I did so. He couldn't take his eyes off them.

"What you drinking, Kate?" Benny asked.

"Whatever he's drinking," I said.

"Tequila it is, then. And you, Sir? Same again?" Finkle nodded without looking at him and didn't notice that Benny was pouring from two different bottles.

"I have to say, Kate," Finkle said, staring at my cleavage, "I always knew you were lovely, but I had no idea *how* lovely. You really are quite beautiful."

"Why thank you, kind Sir," I said, turning on my best southern drawl. "You're not so bad yourself," I lied, and then almost choked on it.

I picked up my glass and downed it in one go.

"Oh boy," I gasped. "I needed that. Same again please, Benny."

I looked at Finkle. The Brits have a word for it, 'Gobsmacked'. That's exactly what he was. I smiled sweetly at him, and put my hand on his knee.

"Are you not drinking, Henry? It is okay for me to call you Henry?"

He nodded, gulped, then grabbed his glass, emptied it, and pushed it across the countertop to Benny, who promptly refilled it, again from the second bottle.

For the next thirty minutes we made small talk together while Benny and Laura kept our glasses full. I was downing mine like I was drinking Sprite, which I was, and all the while pretending to become drunker and drunker. Finkle wasn't pretending. Soon, he was barely holding it together. Me? The drunker he became, the more I encouraged him, led him on. I constantly touched his knee, his hands, once even the inside of his thigh, and as I let my skirt slide higher and higher, his eyes got wider and wider.

Finally, I figured I had him. I leaned forward, placed both my hands on his thighs and leaned in even closer to him, "I need some air," I whispered, my lips brushing his cheek. "How about we go outside for a minute?"

He almost fell off the stool. I took his hand and winked at Benny and Laura. They'd been serving me Sprite and Finkle double measures of tequila, and oh was he drunk.

I led him down the passageway, past the restrooms, and out through the rear door. I pulled him into the space between the dumpster and the rear wall of the Sorbonne. As I did so, I had a flashback; again, I could see Saffron Brooks lying there among the trash—it lasted but a minute and then was gone. I put my arms around Finkle's neck and let him push me back against the wall.

"Oh, Henry," I gasped. "I'm so horny."

I felt him shudder with excitement, "Damn," he slurred. "You're h… horny? I could… I could…" then his lips were on mine, his tongue trying to force its way into my mouth. *Oh my God. The man is going to devour me.*

I kissed him back, passionately; my lips were parted, but my teeth were clamped together, my hands gripping the hair at the back of his head. I felt his hands on my waist, then on my hips, then my buttocks, and then he was pulling me to him. He pressed himself against me and I swear I could literally feel him rising to the occasion, leaving me in no doubt of what he had in mind. I continued to play along. I kissed him like there was no tomorrow. *Thank God he doesn't have bad breath.*

His breathing became harsh, ragged, his hands trembling as he reached down and began to lift my skirt.

Gotcha, you bastard!

Still kissing him hard, I slid my hands from the back of his head to his cheeks, then to his neck. I massaged his skin, feeling for the right spot and then, ever so gently at first, I pressed with both thumbs. It didn't take much—probably because he was so drunk. He went out like a light. His hands dropped to his sides. He slumped against me and began to slide to the ground. I caught him before he hit the concrete and lowered him gently down behind the dumpster. Then I ran inside and yelled to Benny that I was ready. He grinned at me and gestured for Laura to join us.

"Quick," I said. "We have only a minute before he comes to."

It didn't take that long. I unzipped his pants, dragged them down around his knees, then yanked down his shorts, pulled up his shirt, posed him a little, and then... *Oh, m'God, now I know why they call him Tiny!*

He began to stir, and it was then that we left, in a hurry. We entered the Sorbonne, turned and closed the door, almost, then together, the three of us watched through the small opening.

He came around slowly at first, sat for a moment, and then he came fully awake with a start. His right hand let go of the bottle he'd been holding—that I'd placed in his hand—and went straight to his head. He looked up at the dumpster, then he began to get it, the predicament he was in, and he fearfully looked around. Then, with a yell, he realized he was half-naked. He looked around wildly, somehow scrambled to his feet, hurriedly adjusted his shirt and pulled up his pants, zipped up, and then, well, you just had to be there. It was one of the funniest two minutes I'd ever experienced. It was just too funny.

Finally, he managed to get it together and fully clothed once more, though somewhat disheveled, he ran, sort of. My last view was of him staggering as he rounded the corner, his little legs going nineteen to the dozen.

I fell back against Benny, laughing like an idiot.

"Oh my God," Benny gasped. "Don't you think maybe you were a little too hard on him?"

"The hell she was," Laura giggled. "If it had been me, I would've sliced his nuts off, if I could have gotten hold of them. Wow, they were lit...tle. And his... hahahaha."

Chapter 26

The following morning, not more than a couple of minutes after I entered my office, Chief Finkle flung open the door and stormed in, slamming it behind him.

"Wow, you're in a bad mood," I said, before he could speak.

"You slut!" he yelled.

I looked out of my window to see if anyone had heard him. Fortunately, the incident room was still almost deserted.

"What the hell did you do to me last night?" he yelled.

"Calm down, Henry. You'll give yourself an aneurism," I said, smiling. "What did I do to you? I seem to remember kissing you very passionately, which wasn't supposed to happ…"

"Not that, you silly bitch," he interrupted me. "What the hell did you do to me? I woke up on the freakin' ground, half buck freakin' naked. What did you do?"

"Nothing. I did nothing to you. You got very drunk, as I recall… Oh that," I said. "Well, the kiss was so nice," I lied, "and you were so worked up. Henry, your hands, they were all over me, and then you unzipped yourself and tried to pull up my

234

dress... Henry, you were going to have your way with me. What was I to do? I had to do something and, well, you know. A little pressure in the right spot and my virtue was saved."

"I did not freakin' unz... What did you say? Pressure? Oh my God. You could have killed me."

"Not hardly. I knew exactly what I was doing and you were about to rape me." I was laughing at him as I spoke. And then I wasn't. I was damned angry.

"You son of a bitch. You tried to take advantage of me. You thought you had me, you sad freak. So I..."

"You led me on," he interrupted me.

"You're damned right I did. You want to know why? D'you remember when you told me that better men than me had tried to stop you? Of course you do. You're a damned bully and you abuse your power as a senior police officer. You were sexually harassing me and there was not a damn thing I could do about it. The way you looked at me made my skin crawl, and you were threatening my career; hell, you bastard, you even touched me, and then you made those calls, and that was when I knew I had to."

"Had to? Had to what?" he snarled.

"Stop you, you stupid, nasty little man, and when I say *little,* I do mean little. You want to see what I mean?"

Before he could answer, I picked up my iPhone, tapped the screen, opened the first photo and showed it to him. His mouth dropped opened and shut, and then began to work soundlessly. I was reminded of a goldfish.

He was stunned.

"Oh! My! God!" he spluttered. "You, you, you freakin' bitch."

The photo showed him on his ass, slumped against the wall, his pants around his ankles, his left hand at his crotch clasping his tiny member, his right holding the bottle.

"It's a good likeness, don't you think?" I asked.

He shook his head, his mouth opening and closing, speechless.

"How about this, then?" I asked.

I touched the screen and started the video running, then turned it so that we both could see it. He gasped so loud I thought he was having a heart attack; he wasn't."

"You... you lousy slut," he spluttered. "You'll p... pay for this. I'll have your job."

"Oh, I don't think so," I said, gently. "In fact... oh, look at that," I said, holding the phone so he could see it.

The video had not quite reached the point where he was beginning to wake up. I'd been very careful how I shot the footage. He could be seen slumped against the wall, straddled by the longest pair of legs in Chattanooga. The legs—they framed his head and chest—were wearing stiletto heels. Then, whoever they belonged to—no, they weren't mine—dropped his open wallet onto his naked belly, his badge and ID showing. The legs stepped away and he began to stir, then the video showed his right hand grasping a half-empty bottle of cheap tequila; his left hand holding his... Well, you get the idea. Yes, it looked like the assistant chief had gotten himself drunk and then robbed by a long-legged hooker, which was of course, Laura, only she's no hooker.

"It's over, Henry," I said, before he had a chance to speak. "If you ever touch me again, threaten me, make just one suggestive remark—if you even look sideways at me—these photos and video will hit the airwaves so fast it will make you dizzy. Have you got it?" I turned the phone so I could see the screen. Then I looked again at him, "I hope so, because you wouldn't want anyone to see this, especially your wife or the chief, now would you? Oh, and I forgot about the media. My, how they would love to get their hands on it. Would you like to see how easy it would be?"

I tapped the screen a couple of times then hit 'send'. There was a whoosh. I set the phone down on my desk and stared at him, waiting. A few seconds later I heard a weird noise, like an old-timey car horn.

He took his phone from his pocket, stared at it, tapped it once, and scrolled through the screen. His face slowly turning red, and then redder.

"You wouldn't," he growled, now fully with the program. "You wouldn't get away with it. It's all... it's obviously staged. No one would believe it."

I shrugged, "Maybe, maybe not. Are you willing to take that chance?"

He wasn't.

"It's not over, Lieutenant," he snarled. "You'll see," then he stood and stomped out through the door, slamming it behind him.

Chapter 27

It was late afternoon the Monday after the arrest when I happened to be looking out of my office window and laid eyes on Janet Toliver seated at her desk. I smiled to myself, picked up the phone, and asked her to join me.

"Take a seat, Janet," I said. "I need to talk to you."

"Oh dear. Something's wrong... You're going to send me back, aren't you?" she asked with a sad look on her face.

"No. That's not it at all."

"What, then?"

"What did Chief Johnston tell you when he sent you to me?"

"Just that I was to work with you. That's all."

"Well, that's not quite what he told me," I paused, smiled at her, letting the moment build, then I put her out of her misery.

"He said you were to be my new partner. Congratulations Detective Toliver, partner."

For a moment, she sat there, wide-eyed, not comprehending, and then it hit her, "*What?* What did you say? Oh, m'God. I... I, don't know what to say."

"Don't say anything. Go home, have a good evening, and I'll see you here, bright and early, tomorrow morning. Now, get out of here. I need to tidy up a bit."

She backed out of the door, the smile on her face, almost cutting it in two. She was one happy detective. And so was I.

Chapter 28

Over the next several weeks I, that is we, continued to build our case against Lawrence Jackson and MaryJo Hooks.

The DNA profile of the saliva sample taken from the fragments of cigarette paper found on Saffron Brooks was a match to that of MaryJo Hooks, which may sound conclusive, but it wasn't. We knew that the dog was responsible for those, so they didn't physically connect MaryJo to the body, or to any of the others. They were circumstantial evidence. They did, however, provide direct physical evidence that Saffron Brooks had been in the house, naked, and on the rug covered with dog hairs and fragments of paper. That and the matching tire imprints were enough for the district attorney to charge them both with the kidnapping and first-degree murder of all three girls. Unfortunately, there was nothing to link them to either the Perez or Pew murders, so those cases remain open.

Jackson admitted nothing, refusing to talk to anyone, including his court-appointed attorney. After a trial that lasted for ten days, he was found guilty on all charges and sentenced to twenty-five years to life for each of the three murders, and the same again for the kidnappings. In all, Larry

Jackson would be in prison for more than one hundred and fifty years. He could kill no more.

MaryJo, in a separate trial, faced the same charges, but was found not guilty of first degree murder. She was, however, found guilty of aiding and abetting him in his endeavors, which could have carried the same sentences. The theory being that, even though she was tortured and coerced, she had a choice: she could have turned him in at any time—she didn't. A sympathetic judge sentenced her to five to ten years in prison.

Sadie May? She went home with me. I still have her. I managed to cure her of her addiction and she is now the sweetest little friend I ever had, other than Harry Starke, of course.

"But we don't talk about that, do we, Sadie May?" I said as I picked her up and set her on my lap.

The End

Thank you for taking the time to read Saffron, the second book in the new spin-off series of novels featuring Lieutenant Kate Gazzara. If you're familiar with the Harry Starke novels, you already knew who Kate was. If not, well maybe you'd like to read them too – there are twelve of them so far. If so, you can pick up a copy for free by clicking this link: Get Harry Starke. Or you can copy and paste it: http://bit.ly/2gJjQ4M

If you did enjoy Saffron, please consider telling your friends, and post a short review on Amazon (just a sentence will do). Word of mouth is an author's best friend and much appreciated.

Reviews are so very important. I don't have the backing of a major New York publisher. I can't afford to take out ads in magazines and on TV. But you can help get the word out.

To those of my readers who have already posted reviews for this novel and my others, thank you for your past and continued support.

If you have comments or questions, you can contact me by email at blair@blairhoward.com, and you can visit my website:

http://www.blairhoward.com

Thank you. —Blair Howard.